MY SMALLTOWN C.E.O. SCROOGE

A FESTIVE ROMANTIC COMEDY

HARMONY KNIGHT

Copyright © 2020 by Harmony Knight

All rights reserved.

No part of this book may be reproduced in any form or by any electronic or mechanical means, including information storage and retrieval systems, without written permission from the author, except for the use of brief quotations in a book review.

CHAPTER 1

Allie

"Lottie! Emma! Your uncle's here, it's time to go!"

My two giggling nieces come running through from the kitchen with my boss, Bet, who is smiling broadly as she carries a tray of fresh-baked cookies in her hands. Bet's owned this little diner for decades, and aside from Town Hall and the church, it's probably the closest thing this town has to a landmark.

"Uncle Eddie!" the girls squeal simultaneously, filling up the diner with their childish joy as they grab around my brother's legs. Lottie is six, Emma three, and they're the most adorable little girls you could imagine. They remind me of their mother, Libby, every day. And every day I miss her more.

"Mommy!" says Lottie, turning her big, blue eyes up to me. "Bet said we can have cookies but only if you say yes."

"Cookie!" squeals Emma, making grabby hands up at Bet. Her blond curls bounce around her face and I look up to Bet, whose eyes are sparkling at me above her chubby, rosy cheeks.

"Well, all right," I say, to a chorus of squeals and cheers. "But only one. And you'd better tell Aunt Sadie you already had a treat today."

"We will," says Lottie, drawing a little cross over her heart. Bet hands over the cookies—they're huge, practically as big as the girls' heads—and quiet descends on the diner, broken only by the sound of munching and the occasional theatrical "mmmmmmmmm!"

"Thanks for taking them," I say to Eddie, finally getting a chance to hug him good morning. He and his wife, Sadie, look after the girls at least a few times a week for me to work. They never say no, never ask anything in return, and I'm more grateful to them than I can say. It's been a struggle since our sister passed.

"Any time, sis. Sadie and the kids love the company anyway. You staying for dinner tonight?"

"If it's all right," I say. By the time I'm done with a full day's shift at the diner, the last thing I'll want to do is cook.

"Always," says Eddie with a wink. He turns to Bet, who is beaming as she watches the girls devour her cookies. "The place is looking… pretty festive, Bet."

Bet adores holidays. Any holidays. It's less than two weeks after Halloween and the place is already decked out for Christmas. Pumpkins and cobwebs have been swapped out, holly and twinkling lights have moved in, and there's a huge evergreen in the corner covered in tinsel and Bet's collection of mismatched baubles.

"Well, we want to be sure that Santa knows where to go. Isn't that right, girls?" She asks, winking to Lottie and Emma. The girls nod emphatically, munching on their cookies.

"All right, squirts," says Eddie to the girls, as he pushes open the door. "Let's get going. See you later, Allie!"

"Later!" I say, leaning down to give the girls a flurry of kisses. "Be good for your aunt and uncle."

No sooner has Eddie left, trailed by a gaggle of giggles and crumbs, than my coworker-slash-best-friend, Sam, blows in on a gust of wintry November air. He also happens to be Sadie's brother, which makes him my brother-in-law. What can I say? It's a small town.

"WOW!" he says, looking around at the decorations. "Bet, it's fabulous. It must have taken forever."

"Well, Allie helped, so it took half the time. Come through to the kitchen you two, I've got a surprise."

Sam loops his arm through mine and sashays me towards the kitchen behind Bet. "Morning treasure," he whispers, yawning. "You're on coffee duty."

"Late night?"

"Mmmhmmm," he says, giving me side-eye. "It's Drew's day off today so we stayed up drinking wine and watching old movies."

"Riiiiiight," I say, raising my hands to make exaggerated air quotes, "Watching old movies."

He laughs. "Well... that too, but I didn't want to make you jealous."

"Hah!" I snort. "As if! You can't be jealous of things you can't remember."

I'm only very slightly exaggerating. I haven't so much as been kissed by a man since before Libby died, and now that I have full custody of my nieces, they're my life. The idea of dating on top of working enough jobs to keep a roof over our heads is exhausting. And that's before you factor in all the complications that would arise if I *did* hit it off with someone. How could I bring someone new—someone who might not be around forever—into the lives of two little girls who've already lost so much?

"Maybe it's about time you got back on the horse, so to speak," Sam suggests, sticking his tongue out at me.

"Pffft," I blow, dismissively. "Not likely. I know every guy in Sunrise Valley, population seven hundred, and I'm not interested in any of them."

"I'm not saying you have to marry them, but surely there's at least one who could help you… sweep away your cobwebs?" he replies, glancing down towards my crotch, his lips twitching with a restrained laugh. "Maybe you could take a hint from Bet and string up some twinkling lights down there instead."

I tilt my head back, laughing out loud, and pull him into a tight hug. "Love you, Sam."

He fixes me with a serious look, but I can tell he's barely holding himself together. "Oh, Allie. I'd love to help you out, but… you're really barking up the wrong tree here, honey."

We both dissolve into gales of laughter, just as Bet comes back into the room. She flashes us a puzzled smile.

"What'd I miss?"

"Nothing, Bet," I say, wiping the tears from my eyes. "Just Sam being Sam. What's this surprise you have for us?"

She beams at me, thrusting a pile of clothes towards us."Oh, no. Bet! Oh no," I groan, as I realize what she's holding.

"Oh, yes!" she nods, eyes sparkling.

"Oh *yes!*" says Sam, clapping his hands together. He rushes over to unload Bet's arms, handing me a red plaid apron, a pair of reindeer antlers, and a red ball.

"What the…" I say, squeezing the ball.

"It's a nose," says Bet, grinning.

"Oh my God." I stand there staring down at the festive additions to my uniform, shaking my head. I like Christmas as much as the next girl—okay, maybe not as much as Bet, but as much as most girls. But antlers and a Rudolph nose? While serving customers? All of whom are people I meet around town every day?

"Call be Bister Christbas," says Sam, his nose blocked by the squeeze of the red ball. I burst out laughing when I look at him, shaking my head with a smile on my face. The whole situation is too ridiculous to resist.

"The things I do for you, woman!" I tell Bet ruefully. She just stands there, arms folded over her ample bosom, grinning in a way that leaves no doubt that she absolutely, positively expects me to wear this ridiculous get-up.

I pull my apron, antlers, and nose on while Sam makes coffee and Bet fires up the fryers and grill. Within an hour the morning rush is upon us, and we're serving takeout coffees and sit-down breakfasts to all the regulars. All people I know from a lifetime of living in Sunrise Valley.

❄

"There's a new guy out there," says Sam, bustling into the kitchen with a tray in each hand. He starts unloading as I go to peek out through the porthole in the kitchen door.

"Oh, he's handsome," I comment, appreciatively.

The new guy in question is a stranger, and obviously from out of town. He's standing beside a table, taking off his black wool coat and chunky-knit mustard scarf. He's tall—at least six feet—with a smattering of stubble and intensely dark eyes, and even from the other end of the diner, his face looks like it was chiseled from marble by Michelangelo himself. But his expression is hard, and it looks like his mind is a million miles away.

"Doesn't look very happy, though," I comment.

"Pfft, who needs happy when you look like that?" says Sam, appearing beside me to look out the porthole.

"You're leering," I say to him.

"No I'm not!" protests Sam, continuing to leer.

"Is there a man?" asks Bet, squeezing in between us. "Oooh, very nice."

It's at just this moment, with the three of our faces crammed into the little porthole window straining to catch a glimpse, as though the appearance of a good-looking stranger in Sunrise Valley is a rare cosmic event like an eclipse or Halley's comet—and to be fair, it's not far off—that he glances over towards us. We all give a high-pitched yelp and scramble away from the window in unison.

I'm still trying to regain my composure and reassure myself that he definitely didn't see us, when Sam taps me on the shoulder. His grin is even wider than when he saw the reindeer costume this morning.

"It's yoooooour tuuuuuuuuurn," he practically sing-songs.

I groan. Apart from the two years that I was away at art school, I've worked in this diner since I was seventeen. Sam has worked here that whole time, too. I don't remember when it started, but any time a stranger comes in we take it in turns to serve them. With the stipulation that the other gets to make a dare.

"Fine," I say, squeezing my red nose on tighter. I already look ridiculous. How much worse could it get?

"Hmm, let me think," says Sam, looking out of the little round window again and tapping his chin thoughtfully.

"Well, whatever it is you'd better hurry," pipes up Bet. "You two are paid to serve, not think."

"Betty Boop," says Sam. "I would never let you down." He has her wrapped around his little finger and he knows it. As soon as he says it she rolls her eyes, but a smile lifts the corner of her mouth as she turns to take something out of the oven.

"Okay." Sam turns back to me. "Convince him you're French."

"French," I repeat, deadpan.

"Yup!" he nods, looking delighted with himself. In fairness, it's not as bad as the time he had to convince a stranger he was a neurosurgeon moonlighting as a server.

"Fine. Oui, oui!" I say, and Sam grins, rubbing his hands together gleefully like some kind of supervillain. I grab my pen and head out through the door. Sam follows behind me, taking up a position at the far end of the diner from where he can watch my ritual humiliation.

Up close, the stranger is even hotter. He still doesn't smile, not even when he looks up at me in my ridiculous outfit and

I give him the brightest smile I can muster. His eyes flick from my red nose to my antlers and back down, and he says nothing. I decide to brand him as "brooding", since he's probably just passing through town anyway, and it sounds better than "miserable."

"Bonjour!" I say, loud enough for Sam to hear.

Brooding Stranger doesn't flinch.

"Breakfast roll, please," he says, his accent unreadable. He looks pristine in dark jeans, brown brogues and a light blue sweater with the sleeves rolled up. "Eggs over easy."

"Oui, oui!" I say, nodding enthusiastically. "And ehhh, you would like ze tea, or ze coffee?"

I hear Sam snort behind me. Brooding Stranger's eyes flick over to where Sam stands, but I can't turn around to look at him or I'll lose it.

"Coffee," says Brooding Stranger, looking back at me.

"I see, I see," I say, writing his order down. "'Ow about a littol créme?" I pronounce it the way it's pronounced in créme brûlée, and I hear a gasp from behind me and the sound of Sam's feet rushing back towards the kitchen.

The door is still flapping open as he lets out a howl of laughter. Brooding Stranger looks to the kitchen, slowly lifts a brow, and looks up to me. I smile back at him blandly while I suck in on my own throat to stop myself laughing.

"No cream," he says.

"Uno momento!"

Shit, that's Spanish! I rush back to the kitchen as quickly as my feet will carry me. In between deep gulps of air and hysterical laughter, Sam is telling Bet about my attempt to make

Brooding Stranger think I'm French. She's chuckling along with him, shaking her head, the way a mother does when she's trying to hide her amusement at her children's antics.

"I just said 'Uno momento!'"

They both stare at me. Sam gives a little shrug as if to ask "so?"

"That's *Spanish*!" I exclaim, pushing Brooding Stranger's order onto the pass. They both break out in laughter again.

The rest of Brooding Stranger's stay is pretty uneventful. I take him his breakfast, he finishes his entire plate and takes a refill of coffee, and I manage not to say anything else Spanish to him. By the time he finishes up, I'm feeling pretty confident that my charade has managed to convince him.

"Miss," he calls, waving me over. "Check, please."

"Sure thing," I say, distracted, forgetting I'm supposed to be French. "Uh." I put the accent on again. "I will get ze check." Shit, that might have given the game away.

He pays up and leaves a generous tip. When I go back to collect his empty coffee cup, he's on his feet, coat on, wrapping his scarf back around his neck.

"Madame," he begins, and I feel a strange tingling sensation crawling up every one of my limbs. It's not just that he's standing there, towering over me and looking sensationally, unethically delicious. It's that I can somehow sense what's coming.

"Merci pour le repas, c'était délicieux. Il faudra que je revienne. Au revoir." he says, and the very first hint of a smile passes across his lips as he turns to leave. A cold blast of wind from outside blows my hair around my face, and Sam is in fits of hysterics behind me.

"Oh my God," he says, as I watch Brooding Stranger get into a gorgeous, vintage-looking car across the street. *"He speaks French!"*

Sam is weak with laughter, doubled over and leaning on a nearby table. So I take advantage of his weakness and land a towel snap right on his hiney.

CHAPTER 2

Greyson

"Take the next left."

At the sound of the GPS system's command, I slow down and lean forward over the steering wheel, looking around for an off-road. Sunrise Valley sure is a pretty town, but nestled in upstate New York it feels about ten degrees colder than Manhattan did when I left this morning.

"What the…" I put the brakes on and come to a halt opposite an old iron gate that's half buried in overgrown brush. The hedges on either side are almost as tall as the gate itself.

"This can't be it," I mutter, opening my briefcase and riffling through it until I find the document I'm looking for. It's the same gate all right, but in the photo that accompanied the deed it's clear and gleaming with a new coat of paint, and the hedges are low enough that the grand old house can be seen beyond them. There's no way that picture was taken any time in the last twenty years.

"For the love of…" I clench my jaw. This was supposed to be easy. It had been a shock to learn that I had a great aunt I'd never heard of who'd left me her estate in Sunrise Valley, but it wasn't life-changing news. I have enough money already. I'm here to flip it, take the cash and move on.

I root around in the briefcase again and pull out the remote that came with the dossier from my aunt's lawyer. I settle my gaze on the old iron gate and hit the button, fully expecting that nothing will happen.

There's some groaning and some creaking, but sure enough, the gates slowly begin to open. And they keep opening, despite the best efforts of the brambles to hold them back.

"Huh," I say to myself. "Guess they really don't make things the way they used to."

I'm pretty sure my high-tech gate back home would collapse under a stiff breeze. It once flaked out because a bird shat on a sensor, and another time it wouldn't close because a spider had taken up residence in the control box. It took the engineer two hours to figure that out.

Once there's enough room, I turn my car into the driveway and cruise along the winding, tree-lined road until the house comes into view. I'm surprised by how impressive it is. An old Queen Anne with several turrets and intricate spindlework. The paint has faded, but it's clear that it was once a vibrant yellow. The color wouldn't be my first choice, but it gives me a different impression of the late Great Aunt Julia than I've had up 'til now.

The old iron key takes a while to line up inside the lock, and I have to use a bit of force to turn it. As soon as I open the door, one thing is very clear: this will be no easy flip.

A gust of wind sends dust bunnies hopping along the floor, and the air sparkles so much in the afternoon light that it looks like I've just walked into a fantasy film. There's a grand old double staircase in front of me, and whatever furniture I can see is covered in dust sheets.

This is definitely NOT what I signed up for. I reach into my pocket and pull out my phone.

"Call Jacob."

As it rings, I continue looking around, and nothing I see improves my mood. The carpet is old and worn through, the wallpaper is faded and peeling, and the staircase is-

"Greysoooon!" says my lawyer, in his smarmiest city accent. "How are you?"

"Jacob. What the fuck, man?" I demand. I wouldn't speak to just any lawyer that way, but this guy went to the same college as me and we both played on the baseball team. "I just got to this place upstate and it looks like it was abandoned a decade ago."

"Well it was," he says. "Didn't you read the documents I sent along?"

"What? Wait a minute."

I set my briefcase down on top of a sheet-covered side table, sending a puff of dust into the air, and open it up. I find the papers at the very top, still inside the envelope my secretary put them in before I left.

"All right, I've got them."

"Well, it'd be the bit that says your dear old aunt spent the last eight years in elderly care."

I don't say anything for a minute. My mind is too busy taking in my surroundings now that my eyes have adjusted to the light and I can see the full scope of what will need to be done here before I can sell it on. It's not my first rodeo—I just didn't expect there to be quite this much to do.

"Shit," I say under my breath.

"Ah, come on, buddy. You're in marketing, right? Can't you just sell it on as a haunted house or something?"

"You're no help, Jacob," I tell him, and I can hear him reply "Any time, buddy!" as I hang up. He's clearly enjoying this, now that I can't blame it on him anymore.

"Call Ben," I tell my phone. Ben is my secretary, PA, whatever you want to call it. He's the one who keeps the chaos in my life to a minimum. He's well-paid for his position, but he earns every penny—the phone barely rings twice before he answers.

"Hey, boss." He's obviously chewing, and a couple of moments later I hear a loud gulp.

"Am I interrupting lunch?"

"Nope. Just finished. How's uh…" I hear him click his mousepad a couple of times. "Sunny Valley. Sunny?"

"Sunrise. And it's cold," I say. "Listen. The house up here is a bit of a wreck so I'm going to need you to clear my in-office meetings for a while. Change whatever you can to online and push whatever else back."

"Sure thing," he says. "When will I push to?"

I pace across the hall and open a door that leads into a huge room with an open fireplace and yet more dust-sheet-covered furniture. My gaze settles on a pill bug that's crawling across the floor, and I sigh.

"Let's say after Christmas. But schedule me a few days in the office for anything pressing."

"Will do. Flights?"

"Please."

"You need accommodation in Sunrise Valley?"

I think back to this morning, and the cute girl with her little antlers and her red nose, and her hilariously fake French accent. If that had been a motel instead of a diner I might take Ben up on his offer to book me a room, just for the chance at a one-nighter with her.

"No. I can stay in the house. Thanks."

"Any time," says Ben as I hang up.

❄

Within the hour I've been around every room in the house. Dust sheets, disrepair, and creepy crawlies aside, it's really a beautiful building. If it was near the city I might keep it. Alas, it's in the ass-end of bumfuck nowhere and the only entertainment seems to be a bar that has the occasional singer. Aside from the French reindeer girls, of course.

I take the dust sheets off some of the furniture in the kitchen, one of the bedrooms, a bathroom, and one of the reception rooms so that I can at least live here for the time being. But there's a lot to do and there's no way one man is going to do it all alone by Christmas. I need some help.

I manage to light the range without setting the whole house on fire, and boil enough water to make myself a coffee with the small sachet of instant I pocketed on the plane. It's not the finest freeze-dried bean I've ever tasted, but it's warm and it hits the spot.

Settled on a sofa with a blanket around me and coffee in hand, I open my laptop. Fortunately, cell coverage is pretty good here, and my data plan means that I can use my phone to get online—I really doubt that Great Aunt Julia left a WiFi router hiding in any of these rooms. I head straight to Help-ForHire.com and type in my location. No matter where I've been in the country, no matter what work I've needed doing, this site has never failed me yet. I hit enter, and whereas in New York City there are pages and pages of all sorts of people with all sorts of specialist skills, in Sunrise Valley there is precisely one person registered.

"Alora Brooks," I say to no-one in particular, "I guess you're my only choice."

```
Ms. Brooks

I have need of services to include clean-
ing, light repairs and decorating, to begin
as soon as possible. Please reply with your
availability and hourly rate.

Regards,

G. Blair
```

Message sent, I open up my favorite playlist, settle back with my eyes closed, and take a moment to relax. Maybe this will be an adventure. Maybe a few weeks away from the city will do me good. My brother's always telling me to take time off, and his admonitions that I work way too much are not entirely unwarranted.

My mind wanders back to the diner this morning. It had that small-town charm, but I wasn't expecting to see someone as stunning as Reindeer Girl there. Those big, green eyes, dark, curly hair falling out of a topknot. Perfectly curvy, perfect height, and a sense of humor. Even with the ridiculous Christmas outfit on I could tell she was smoking underneath. My mind wanders a little more, imagining what she looks like without the nose and antlers… without clothes… then without clothes but with the nose and antlers... There's a twitch in my pants and I reach down under the blanket, only to be pulled out of my daydreams when my laptop pings at me.

Ben, maybe? It's after 8 pm, but he reliably ignores me whenever I tell him to stop working so late. I reach for the laptop and read the notification: I have one new message on HelpForHire.


```
G. Blair

Thank you for your message. I'd be
delighted to work for you. My hourly rate
is $20 and I am available on Tuesdays,
Thursdays, and Fridays, plus occasional
weekends. Evenings are negotiable but will
require advance notice and will be charged
at $30 per hour.

I am able to start tomorrow.

Regards,

Alora Brooks
```

. . .

```
Sometimes you never know the value of a
moment until it becomes a memory.
```

The last line is written in some kind of purple Comic Sans-like font and I blink as I read it. Twice. The idea that someone has that as their signature, let alone for work-related emails, makes me feel like I've stepped into a parallel universe. But what choice do I have? There is quite literally no other help for hire in this weird dimension full of dusty old mansions, Parisian reindeer girls, and emailed platitudes.

```
Ms. Brooks

Please bring your resume along tomorrow at
10 am sharp. The address is Sunrise Valley
House, on Old Green Road.

Regards,

G.Blair.
```

I don't even get a chance to settle back onto the couch before the laptop pings again.

```
G. Blair

Great! See you then. And thanks.

Regards,

Alora Brooks
```

. . .

```
Sometimes you never know the value of a
moment until it becomes a memory.
```

I don't know why that signature bothers me so much, but I spend another long moment staring at it, lips pursed like an old fisherwoman.

"Scotch," I say to myself, decisively, and rise from the sofa to retrieve the bottle of Glenmorangie that I packed for this trip.

If nothing else, this is going to be an interesting few weeks.

CHAPTER 3

❄

Allie

I thought I'd left plenty of time to get everything done this morning, but the second I step outside with the girls and see my car, shimmering in the morning light with a thick layer of frost all over it, all I can do is sigh.

"Shit," I say.

"Shit!" says Emma.

"That's a bad word, Mommy," notes Lottie, frowning up at me with her little arms folded.

"Uh. Yeah. Don't say shi… that," I tell Emma, half distracted as I try to pull open the car door. It barely budges, and the ominous crackle of frost confirms my worst suspicions.

"Told you it was a bad word," says Lottie, sticking out her tongue at her younger sister.

"Back inside!" I tell the girls, ushering them towards the front door.

By the time I've covered my car in enough warm water to bathe an elephant, managed to pry the doors open and turn on the internal heaters to clear the rest of the frost, retrieved the girls and got them strapped in, and collected my bag from the kitchen, I'm afraid to check the time.

So when Emma looks at me with a very worried expression on her face, just as I'm putting on my seatbelt, and mutters the words "poop, Mommy," it's difficult not to take it as a statement on how this day is going so far.

One whirlwind bathroom visit later, I turn the key to start the engine and the CD player starts blasting The Wheels on the Bus at me. Usually, I switch to my phone input before starting the car so that I can listen to a podcast during the drive, but once the girls have heard the first note of a kids' song I have no chance. They will stage a protest in the back seat if I even think about changing it.

A glance at the clock tells me it's 9:53 am.

"SHIT."

"Shit!" calls Emma.

"Mommyyyy!" protests Lottie, sounding genuinely offended.

"Don't say that word!" I call to Emma, who's already moved on to singing The Teddy Bear's Picnic and can barely hear me over the sound of her own voice.

We reach Eddie's house in record time. I practically eject the girls from their seats and throw them at my sister-in-law, Sadie, who's waiting at the door.

"My, you're certainly in a hurry today!" Sadie remarks as I shower the girls with kisses.

"SUPERLATEGOTTAGOLOVEYOUALL!" I call as I wave-sprint back to the car. I put the pedal to the metal and arrive at the open gates of Sunrise Valley House less than ten minutes later.

Crawling up the winding driveway I can see the familiar old house coming into view, and I feel a little flutter of excitement. I've spent my life driving past the place, but I've never been up to the house before. A few months ago, when news reached Sunrise Valley that the previous occupant had died, Bet told me that old Ms. Blair used to live here alone and go into the town every Saturday for cake and tea at the diner, and every Sunday for church. A big place for one widow with no children, she'd said, and wondered out loud what would become of it now. I guess I'm about to find out.

Cleaning, light repairs, and decorating. That was what the message said. Well, I can do the cleaning for sure. The light repairs might be a stretch, but how hard can it be, really? And I've given rooms a lick of paint before. In any case, I wasn't about to say no with Christmas just around the corner and two little girls' faces to put smiles on.

I fluff my curls in the rearview, grab my bag, and jump out of the car. As I jog toward the door, I glance at my phone. Thirteen minutes late. Well, at least I didn't break any mirrors or walk under any ladders on my way here. Silently hoping that my new employer has a flexible definition of "sharp," I ring the bell and start rooting around in my bag for my resume. I'm still trying to dig it out as the loud BING BONG of the old-school bell fades away and I hear the door creak open.

"You're late."

The voice is deep and deadpan. For some reason, I'd expected a woman.

"I'm so sorry!" I say, finally fishing out my resume. There is less bag-fluff attached to it than I expected, but it's a little crumpled so I pull at the edges to straighten it out. "I promise it's a one-off. I wasn't expecting the frost so I had to get the ice off the car before I set out." Resume straightened out, I hand it over. "It won't happen ag—"

Oh. My. God. It's him. Brooding Stranger. My heart jumps right up into my throat as I lock eyes with the guy from the diner, suddenly wondering how on Earth I didn't put two and two together sooner. I do also briefly wonder if it's too late to start affecting a French accent again.

"Come in," he says. There's no smile on his face. Not even a hint of one. But there is that slight sparkle of amusement in the depths of his dark brown eyes, the same as yesterday when he reeled off his French before leaving.

He turns and walks inside, holding my resume in front of him as he thumbs through it. I step into the large entrance hall and close the door behind me. Looking around the foyer, I can see that this house must have been something special in its prime. It's a grand old place. It's full of dust and there are still sheets on half the furniture, but grand nonetheless.

I settle my gaze back on Brooding Stranger, who is studying my resume like it's the constitution or something, and the silence begins to feel itchy on my skin.

"So you must be related to Ms. Blair," I say, a little too eagerly.

He glances up, his dark eyes pinning me to the spot, and I swallow.

Look. He's hot, okay? Like, model hot. And a girl can look. And if a swarm of butterflies takes flight in my tummy, so what? He's just blowing through town, and he's something different to all the men I've seen here my whole life.

"Mmhmm," he says, eventually, and his voice is a low rumble. "Apparently."

"Apparently?" I ask, curiosity piqued.

"Mmhmm," he says, looking back down at the paper, and I'm immediately irritated by how little he says. He must be a city boy.

"Right," I say, folding my arms and looking around the hall.

I sense him looking at me again and turn to face him. His eyes flick up to mine, as though he were looking elsewhere.

"Children?" he asks.

"Huh?"

"Do you have children?"

Lord, forgive me, but my car broke down last month, the repair drained my savings account, and I really need the money from this job if I'm going to give the girls any sort of Christmas. Plus he seems like the type who'd turn me down if I said yes. And it's not really a lie anyway, is it? I've never given birth to any children.

"Nope," I say, shaking my head.

He drops my resume onto a table and nods.

"Husband? Boyfriend?"

"Uh. Not sure that's any of your business?" I say, a little astonished he even asked. Is that legal?

He looks me up and down, his face unreadable, and nods again.

"True. Come through."

I follow him through the entrance hall and into one of the reception rooms where someone—presumably him—has made camp. The dust sheets have been pulled off a large, bottle green couch with embroidered arms and a coffee table. There's a blanket on the couch and a laptop, a notepad, and an empty mug on the table.

Out of habit, I pick up the mug from the table straight away. When I turn around, he's staring at me again.

"It's polished," I say.

He looks at me like I may be insane.

"The table," I tell him, wafting my hand to it. "You'll make rings."

He's quiet again, looking from me to the table to the mug and then back to me. He pulls a dust sheet from the chair on the opposite side of the coffee table, sending a cloud of fresh dust flying into the air, and nods toward it for me to sit. So I do. With the mug in my hands.

"I'm Mr. Blair," he says. Very formal. "I'll be here for a few weeks. As you may have deduced, I inherited this house from my great aunt. I intend t—"

"Did you know her?" I ask. "Bet says she used to come into the diner when she still lived here, but I didn't work there then."

"No," he says. And that, it seems, is that. "Anyway, there's plenty to do here. I'll make a list of jobs whenever you come by. I don't have one today because I haven't been through the place yet, but you can help me remove the dust sheets and air the place out."

"Right," I say, a little too late. I got distracted by the shapes his mouth makes when he talks. He really is quite stunning.

"How long do you have today, Alora?"

"*Ms. Brooks*," I correct him. It's petty, but if he's enforcing formality then so will I. There's a small twitch at the corner of his mouth and I swear he almost smiles.

"Ms. Brooks," he nods. I regret it immediately. There's something particularly sexy about him referring to me that way. Very My Fair Lady. "How long do you have today?"

"A few hours," I say. "I need to be back in town by two."

"To work at the diner?" he asks.

I raise a brow at him. He's nosy. He just stares placidly back at me.

"No," I say, shaking my head, and we stare at each other in stubborn silence for a while... until what I presume is a grandfather clock suddenly BONGS loudly from under a sheet right behind me and I nearly jump out of my skin.

"Jesus shit!"

My whole body jerks, including my hands and the mug I'm holding, which sends a couple of drops of the cold coffee mud splashing onto my face. I'm pretty sure I hear him snort a laugh, but by the time I look back up he's already on his feet beside me.

"That thing scared me last night, too," he says. His eyes are a little softer and he's holding a handkerchief. He stands over me and reaches down, dabbing gently at my cheek. There's something tender about the way he does it, and something intense about this sudden intimacy with someone who is, let's face it, an absolute stranger.

"Do you have any other jobs?" he asks. I'm so distracted by the tingling sensation on my cheek that I almost miss the question.

"No," I say, shaking my head. "Wait. I mean yes. I work at Jimmy's bar sometimes. That's evenings though, usually."

He nods and takes the mug out of my hands, placing it down on the table.

"We'll work out your schedule later," he says. "And you can invoice me through HelpForHire at the end of each week, all right?"

He doesn't wait for an answer. "Come on, we'll get started with the dust sheets."

I nod and stand, but before I follow him out of the room I reach for the mug on the table, pick it up from the polished wood again, and set it down on top of his notepad. If he gets a ring on there it's his own fault for not having coasters.

"Ms. Brooks?" he calls from the hall. I quickly pull my sleeve down over my hand, swipe it across the coffee ring on the tabletop until it's gone, and follow him out.

CHAPTER 4

Greyson

It's the first day of my second week in Sunrise Valley, on a house-flipping project that is supposed to be on a tight deadline, and I've been pacing in the kitchen for the past twenty minutes. I have plenty I could be getting on with; emails, calls, looking over my company's ongoing projects. But I get this nervous energy whenever Ms. Brooks is due to arrive, and I just can't bring myself to sit still. It's a little pathetic, but no-one besides me will ever know.

I shouldn't have asked her whether she had a husband or boyfriend during our first meeting last week. Very unprofessional. And it's probably for the best that she didn't answer me. Knowing me, I'd probably have pursued her for a one-night stand, but there's something about her that makes me think a quick roll on the couch wouldn't have scratched the itch the way it usually does. I'd have wanted more, and since my ironclad rule is that I don't do more, that would have been disastrous. So I'll keep my distance, be as brief as I can when I talk to her, and let her think whatever she wants about me.

What she probably thinks about me is that I'm a standoffish asshole. Which, again—good thing. I don't do relationships, and that's for the best. For me, and for the women I might have ensnared if I'd wanted to. And it's definitely best for gorgeous, faux-French smalltown girls with dazzling smiles and an overabundance of consideration for coffee tables.

"BING BONG!"

The doorbell rings just as the kettle starts to whistle on the range. I pick it up, put it down to one side, and go to answer the door.

"Morning!" Alora is smiling, standing there in jeans and boots, a thick coat, a chunky scarf, and a rainbow-colored woolly hat with a bobble on the top and what I think is a Care Bears patch sewn onto the side. She looks ridiculous. And adorable.

"Nice hat," I say, nodding to it.

She gives me a wider grin and plucks it off her head, releasing a mop of dark curls that bounce all around her lovely face. At some point since she first started working here, she must have realized that she was the only person in town registered on HelpForHire, because she's gotten a lot more talkative and a lot less awkward since that first day. Not that I'm complaining.

"Couldn't find mine so I had to borrow my niece's. What's that smell?"

She's walking forward, face lifted, sniffing as she goes. I loft a brow at her and move out of the way, watching her go another couple of steps before she turns around, still sniffing. She's like a bloodhound on a trail. Ridiculous. And adorable.

I fold my arms over my chest and continue to watch her. She gets closer and then a little closer again, and then she leans right into me, pressing lightly against my front. My breath hitches when I feel the tip of her November-cold nose against my neck. I freeze, feeling a distinct, instant twitch in my pants.

"It's you!" she says, stepping back. She's lucky I don't grab her up in her stupid coat and carry her upstairs. "Nice cologne."

I turn away from her and walk with some difficulty back to the kitchen, placing myself strategically behind the breakfast bar, which—thankfully—is waist-high. The last thing I need is to end up on some sort of registry.

"Hot date," I say, sardonically.

Because I've been restraining myself so carefully around her, she doesn't pick up on the sarcasm. "OoooOOH!" she says, her voice lilting up and down. "Who's it with? No, no. Let me guess."

I'm not about to stop her.

"Coffee?" I ask. She nods, but her finger is tapping against her chin as she looks me over.

"Let's see. Emily from the bar? No. Too young. Hmm…"

I put the kettle back on the range to regain a little heat and pull a coffee press out of the cupboard overhead. Much better than the instant crap I had to drink the first night.

"Amanda from the post office?" she asks. "She's kind of older than you though. Do you like cougars?"

I fix her with a look, but she's oblivious. She pushes herself onto one of the high stools on the other side of the island and puts her Care Bears hat down on the counter.

"Ohhh. Samantha would be a good fit for you. Samantha Reynolds. She's pretty, blond, blue eyes. Works in her father's antique shop on the corner of Main Street. Yeah," she says, nodding. I slide her coffee over to her. "I bet that's it. You went in to look at furniture for this place and your eyes met across a vintage armoire…"

I take a deliberately slow sip of coffee and set my mug down. Then I shake my head.

"There's no date. That was a joke." I can't stop myself adding: "and I'm not into blonds."

She flicks her green gaze up to mine, and our eyes meet for a long moment.

"Sooo," she says, breaking the silence, but not before I've spent far too long thinking about kissing her. "I guess you're pretty bad at jokes?"

I turn around a little too quickly, before my face has a chance to betray me, and pick up my coffee ring-covered notepad from the worktop opposite the island. Opening it to the last page I was writing on, I spin it around and push it toward her.

"This is what's on the agenda for today."

She sips her coffee quietly and reads it over.

"You know," she says, looking up at me. "There's not actually as much to be done as I thought there would be, the first day I came over. Now that all the sheets are off it looks way better. If I get the rest of the dusting done today I bet it'll look great."

She's right. There are definitely trouble spots; paper peeling off the walls, a little dry rot here and there, and the whole place needs a fresh coat of paint and some new fixtures. But compared to a lot of places I've flipped it's not half bad. I don't know why I haven't called Ben and told him I might be done in four weeks instead of six. Or maybe I do know the reason, and she's sitting across the island from me.

"Yeah. It's a nice place."

"You never thought about keeping it?" she asks, her head tilted to one side quizzically. And adorably.

I snort through my nose and shake my head. "Nah. My company's in New York City. What use do I have for a house in the ass-end of—"

Her glare is immediate and devastating and silences me immediately.

"Well, you have to admit. Sunrise Valley is pretty remote."

"Mmm," she says, and sips her coffee. "What's your company do?"

"Marketing," I reply, and I leave it at that. I don't tell her I co-own one of the most successful marketing companies in the city. And with her, it's not even because I'm worried she'll smell money and get weird—I'm pretty sure she's not the type. It's because I don't want her to think that I'm bragging.

"Fun," she says, as though my deadpan, distant way of communicating with her is starting to rub off. I hope that doesn't happen. I'd miss her smile.

"It has its moments. Have you always lived in Sunrise Valley?"

"Yup!" she says, brightening a little. She looks back down to the notepad, tapping her finger on the page. "Lucky for you, judging by the number of contractors you need to bring in."

I feel a bit guilty, having been so dismissive of Sunrise Valley. It's got its charms. I look down at the notepad and move around the counter to stand beside her. She smells like vanilla and some sort of fruit.

"You have all of these in town though, right?" I ask. I'm going to need an electrician, a plumber, a carpenter… the list goes on. I did say I'd flipped houses before—I never said I'd done it single-handed. I'm more of a project manager than an all-purpose handyman.

"Of course. You want me to call them for you?"

I hesitate, looking over the list. And then an idea strikes me, and before I realize how stupid it is, I say it out loud.

"I actually prefer to do business face-to-face. We'll make a full list of what needs doing today, and then maybe you can take me to meet them? Are you free tomorrow?"

It's an abject lie. Nobody prefers doing business by phone and email more than me. It's efficient. And it takes a lot of the emotion out of the equation, which comes in handy when you're trying to convince people to market their beloved products and services in ways they'd never imagined. But I've been here over a week and I've barely left the house. I'm starting to get cabin fever.

"No, not tomorrow. Wednesday, maybe?" she asks. "I work the diner in the morning but my shift is over at noon. I'll have to check my planner…"

"Great. I'll buy you lunch. Call it a bonus."

A ripple of excitement runs up my spine at the thought of taking her to lunch, and once again I have to school my face to stop it from betraying me.

"Last of the big spenders," she murmurs, looking back down at the notepad. But I can see the side of her cheek lifting with a smile.

"Oh," she says, tapping the end of the pen against the paper. "The plumber. Caleb. He's out of town at the moment. I'll call Caroline and see when he'll be back."

"Caroline?" I ask. She looks up, her green eyes framed with dark lashes. God, she's beautiful. Every time her lips move I imagine the most sinful things.

"His wife. She's a friend of mine."

Of course she is. Everyone is a friend of everyone around here, by the looks of it.

"Right," I nod. I reach for the pen, and I feel a jolt as my skin makes contact with hers. She freezes, and I'm suddenly, acutely desperate to know if it's because she felt the same thing.

"Sorry," she mumbles, releasing the pen into my grip and dropping her hand onto her lap. She swallows uncomfortably, and I clear my throat.

"Sorry," I say, and put a little asterisk beside the word "plumber" on the paper.

I take a few steps away to reclaim a little distance and busy myself with rinsing out my coffee cup.

"All right," I say, trying to affect an authoritative air, as though I'm not constantly thrown off my game by her presence. "Let's get moving, shall we? I'll start in the yard and you start upstairs. Just write down any little jobs you see that need doing, and we'll put a list together later. You can use these." I pull a second notepad and another pen out of a nearby cupboard and place them on the countertop in front of her.

"Sure thing," she says, pushing her cup away. She takes the notepad and pen and leaves the room before I can say anything else. Like she feels as much of a need to get away from me as I feel to get away from her. I can't help but wonder, as I watch her go, whether she feels the same pull to get closer.

CHAPTER 5

Allie

"Thanks so much for doing this again, Sadie," I tell my sister-in-law as she hands me a steaming mug of coffee. It's 7:30 am and the girls have run upstairs to see their cousins. Sadie is watching them for me to work a breakfast shift at the diner before I meet Mr. Blair for lunch.

"Hey, any time," she says. "You know that."

I take my first sip and close my eyes, willing the caffeine into my veins. I seem to be living on coffee, these last couple of weeks. When I open my eyes again, Sadie is frowning at me.

"You look tired," she says. "Are you sure you haven't taken on too much?"

I take a deep breath and puff out my cheeks as I sigh it back out.

"Maybe," I admit. "I fell asleep watching a movie with the girls last night. I didn't wake up until midnight and they were both asleep on top of me."

Between my shifts at the diner and the bar, and now the extra work up at the mansion, I've barely had any time to rest. Even when I do have time off, it's spent running errands, stocking up on groceries, and catching up on laundry. If I'm lucky I'll manage to find an hour here and there to give the girls my undivided attention.

It's not sustainable, no matter how much I need the money. I'm exhausted.

"You know, we could loan y—"

"No," I cut her off, a little more harshly than I intended to. The idea of borrowing money from Eddie and Sadie, after all the help they give me with the girls, makes me balk. Plus I know they'd never let me pay them back. "But thank you!" I add, trying to soften my response. "You already do enough, helping with the girls. I don't know what we'd do without you."

"Psht. You're a warrior and you'd do just fine," she says. She really is the most amazing friend. "Besides, they're a pleasure."

"Yeah, they are," I agree. As much work and stress as it is to be responsible for these two little humans, they really do fill up my life and my heart.

"Y'know, Allie, if it's too much, it's too much," she says. "You're raising two wonderful children. You know they'll be happy with whatever you get them for Christmas. Maybe you should think about going a bit easier on yourself."

"Yeah." I nod. It's a fair point. The mansion was only going to be a temporary gig anyway. And if I'm honest, it's been more hours than I was expecting when I took the job. "And Blair will have all the tradesmen he needs after today. There probably won't be much left for me to do."

"Blair is the guy at the mansion?" she asks.

"Mr. Blair," I say. "His name's Greyson. I saw it on a letter up at the house. But he introduced himself as Mr. Blair so…" I shrug.

"Oooh," says Sadie, wrinkling her nose. "Is he all stuffy and pompous?"

I shrug again. He is. And he isn't. It always feels a bit like he's purposely holding back, putting up a front. He's so distant a lot of the time, but he'll occasionally say something dry and funny, and when I laugh his eyes betray a sparkle that makes me think he's smiling on the inside.

"I told him to call me Ms. Brooks," I say, and Sadie laughs.

"Of course you did," she says. "You're the most contrary person I know."

"No I'm no—" I begin, before I realize what I'm saying. Sadie's amused, I-told-you-so expression brings a smile to my face. "Okay, maybe there's *some* truth in that."

Sadie looks like she's just about to argue the "some" in that sentence, but we're interrupted by the sound of my phone ringing. I put my coffee down, dig it out of my bag, and glance at the screen before answering it.

"Hey, Jimmy," I'm surprised to be hearing from him so early, and I don't quite succeed in keeping it out of my voice.

"Allie, hey. How're things?" the voice on the other end replies, sounding a little hesitant.

"All good. What's up?" I say, my brow furrowing. Usually, by this point in our calls, Jimmy is already reeling off a list of extra shifts that he wants me to work.

"Well, uh," he pauses. "The thing is... Jimmy Junior came home yesterday."

Jimmy Junior left town six months ago with nothing but his guitar and a heart full of hope, to try and make it in the city. Jimmy's spent the entire time since fretting that his son would never come home again, and talking my head off about Junior's childhood every chance he gets.

"Oh, that's great!" I say, and despite the fact that I know what's coming, I'm genuinely happy for Jimmy that JJ is home. "You must be so glad to see him."

"Yeah, it's great to have him back," says Jimmy, sounding a little more relaxed. "But he's in need of work, Allie, and I don't think anyone in town is going to take him right away, what with how he left and all. And… well..."

"You're letting me go," I say. Across the table, Sadie rolls her eyes. We both know that every job in a town like Sunrise Valley is forever under threat from a prodigal son, or a sister in need of some extra cash, or a teenage nephew looking for summer work.

"Yeah," Jimmy says, after barely a pause. "Sorry, Allie. But I know you have this new job up at the mansion. And I'll give you the best reference Sunrise Valley ever saw. It's just… family. You know."

"I know, Jimmy," I say.

"No hard feelings?" he asks.

"No hard feelings. Say hi to JJ for me, though, all right?"

"I will, and you be sure to come by and see us, ya hear? Junior's setting up some karaoke thing this Friday. It should be fun. He's full of ideas."

"That *does* sound fun," I say. "See you soon, Jimmy."

"You'd better promise," he says. "Thanks for understanding, Allie. You're a good girl."

I hang up the phone and rub my temples.

"JJ's home?" asks Sadie. It's more of a statement than a question.

"Yup."

"Maybe it's a sign…" she suggests, trailing off.

"Maybe," I concede, picking up my bag as I stand up from the counter. "The pay is better up at the mansion and it's not late nights like the bar, so that's something."

It's only a temporary gig, but to my surprise, I realize I'm quite pleased that I won't be able to quit my job with Mr. Blair after all.

"That's the spirit," says Sadie, setting down her coffee and standing to hug me. "And you'll give Cityboy McGrouchpants as good as you get. I know you will."

❄

"Coming through!" calls Sam as he barges backward through the kitchen doors, carrying a tray full of dirty plates and glasses.

It's been a super busy breakfast shift and my feet are throbbing as I stand at the sink, still scrubbing bits of egg off the last lot of plates Sam delivered. I hope Mr. Blair brings his car because the passenger door of mine doesn't open and the idea of traipsing all over town on sore feet does not fill me with joy.

"This is the last of them," says Sam, emptying the waste into the trash and stacking the plates up beside me. "Thank God. You're off soon, right?"

I nod, rubbing a bead of sweat from my forehead with the back of my wrist. "Yup. I have a few things to do this afternoon, but I guess there's no bar shift tonight so I have some free time."

"I still can't believe Jimmy fired you," says Sam, slapping his hand on his hip and shaking his head.

I shrug. I've gotten used to the idea now. And if I'm honest, the work up at Sunrise Valley House is more interesting and less taxing than herding drunks at the bar. Plus I won't miss the girls' bedtimes anymore.

"It's his son," I say.

"Well. Still," says Sam, all sass. "Does he work as hard as you? No. Can he run a bar like you? No. Nepotism, that's all it is!"

"Sam, we're in Sunrise Valley, not an episode of Law and Order."

"Well. Still!" he says again, heading back to the door. He stops.

"Oh, hey. Isn't that Hotbod McMansion?"

I shake off my gloves in the sink and head over, laughing.

"Is this a thing in your family? Your sister called him Cityboy McGrouchpants this morning."

"He can be as grouchy as he likes, looking like that," he says, wistfully.

"Behave yourself," I say, giving him a good-natured dig in the ribs with my elbow. "You're already spoken for."

I look out through the window and sure enough, there he is. Handsome as ever. All angles and height and moody dark eyes. He's wearing stonewash jeans and the same brown brogues, with a chunky-knit grey sweater. I'm starting to think he has a relative who really, really loves to knit.

"Well I'm sure as shit not calling him Mr. Blair," says Sam. "So formal and stuffy. He *is* hot, though. Just look at him."

I do. And Sam is one thousand percent right, but I'm not going to tell him that.

"Mmhmm," I say, casually, turning away from the door.

Sam immediately gasps and spins around to face me.

"Alora Brooks, do you have a crush on your boss?"

I roll my eyes at him, avoiding the question.

"Bet!" he says, as she comes in from the pantry. He points an accusing finger at me. "She has a crush on Broodyface McStubble!"

"I do not!" I object.

"She does," says Sam, delighted from his nose to his toes. "Look at her, blushing!"

"Leave her alone," says Bet, giving me a wink. "She's only just finished her breakfast shift. If a red face is all it takes to have a crush then we've all got one!"

"He's here," Sam says, beckoning Bet over to the window. "Look!"

I take the opportunity to get away and change, and I hear them giggling away together as I head through to the back.

I change quickly, pulling on a pair of jeans, knee-high black boots, and a bottle-green sweater. I loosen my bun, letting my hair fall around my face, then give my curls a quick squirt of perfume to get rid of the greasy smell that can linger after the end of a shift. That's about as far as I'd usually go, but today I make sure to freshen up my makeup, smear on a thin slick of lip gloss, and brush on a quick coat of mascara.

"Go on and serve him then," I can hear Bet telling Sam when I come out.

"Yeah, Sam," I say as I breeze past them and through the door. "Service please!"

I can't help but grin to myself, imagining the look on their faces in the little round window as they realize he's here to have lunch *with me*.

"Mr. Blair," I greet him as I pull up to the table. He looks up at the mention of his name and immediately gets to his feet when he realizes that it's me.

"Greyson," he says, his eyes almost smiling.

I smile before I can stop myself. "Okay."

"All right if I call you Alora?" he asks.

"Are you my mother?" I ask, sitting down in the seat opposite him. "And also angry at me? Because the only time I get called 'Alora' is when both of those things are true." I grin at him. "Allie is fine."

"Allie," he says, and I enjoy him saying my name more than I expected—I might even prefer it to "Ms. Brooks." I notice that he doesn't sit back down until I've taken my seat, and though I'm sure I'm reading too much into it, this apparent display of old-fashioned chivalry sends a tingle of excitement up my spine.

"I figured we'd just have a quick bite and then take my car to meet the tradesmen."

"Sounds good," I say, picking up a menu and studying it. I know every single item by heart and I could whip any one of them up in a heartbeat, but I still feel the need to distract myself from staring across the table at Greyson while we wait.

"So what's good?" he asks. "You're the expert."

"Bet's Brunch," I say, without hesitation. "Eggs and potato hash, salsa, sausage. And as much coffee as you can handle. It's the best-seller, too."

I sound like I'm giving a sales pitch. It's the exact same patter I give to customers when they ask me for a recommendation, but it also happens to be true. There's a reason Bet's stayed in business her whole life.

"Good afternoon!" says Sam, his voice a sing-song welcome. "Welcome to Bet's."

I glance up and he's looking at me intently, obviously desperate to tease me for not telling him I'd be meeting Greyson here after work. But that would have made it more than it is. It's work. A work thing. Nothing weird about that.

"What can I get for you two?" He attacks Greyson with his most saccharine smile, and Greyson does that thing where he manages to somehow smile by moving only the bottom half of his eyelids. It's really an extraordinary feat.

"Two Bet's Brunches, please," says Greyson. "With coffee."

Wait. Did he... did he just... order *for* me? First names are one thing, but this is altogether too familiar of him. My jaw drops for a split second, and I look up to Sam with steel in my eyes.

"And another one," I say, stubbornly and a little too loudly.

Sam lifts a brow and looks from me to Greyson and back again. When I glance at Greyson he, too, has one brow lifted.

"A- another one?" asks Sam.

"Yes," I say, with an emphatic nod.

"So… three brunches?" he says.

"Yup!"

For a second, Sam looks like he's about to turn around and head back to the kitchen with the order. But as I watch, I can see the doubt creep back into his mind, like it simply cannot believe it really heard the insane thing it just heard.

"Three brunches… for the two of you."

"YUP!" I say. I can feel a flush starting to seep up my neck, so I quickly grab the menu out of Greyson's hand, pair it with mine, shove them both at Sam, and say "Thank you!"

"Ooookay!" says Sam, knowing better than to challenge me when I'm wearing the death stare.

I look up at Greyson and give him a smile like that was completely normal, like people come in here and order double brunch every day. But inwardly, I'm groaning at myself. There's going to be an extra brunch on the table all the way through lunch now, just sitting there, untouched, like a delicious monument to my stubbornness.

❄

Greyson is surprisingly good at small talk. Or at least… he's good at listening to it. Before I know it I've run through the list of tradesmen we need to see, told him who they are, where they live, and how long they've been in Sunrise Valley.

When our lunch arrives, Sam sets the coffee down and very pointedly places the third brunch in the middle of the table, right between myself and Greyson.

"In case you decide you want to share it," he says, clearly delighted at this unexpected chance to mortify me.

"SO," I say to Greyson, trying to ignore Sam's mischievous grin as he turns to leave, "What color do you think you'll paint it?"

"The house?" he asks. "Grey, most likely."

I wrinkle my nose.

"What? What's wrong with grey?"

I shrug, fast-chewing a mouthful of egg until I can swallow it. "Well it's not the most... you know..." I trail off, looking at his grey sweater.

He stares at me, chewing slowly and looking expectant.

"Interesting," I say, and take a sip of coffee. He does that thing again, where his eyes look amused without the rest of his face moving.

"Here," he says, turning his phone to face me. "This is the color I was thinking of."

I give him a so-so shrug as I lift my cup to take a sip of coffee. "I thought the yellow was nice. Vibrant. More... human."

He frowns, turning the phone back around so he can look at it again himself, and just as he opens his mouth to respond, all hell breaks loose.

"MOMMY!"

Lottie slams into my side and wraps her arms around my waist, Emma slams into the back of her, and the shock of the impact sends the coffee that was in my mouth spraying outward, all over Greyson's face and grey sweater.

"Oh, shhhh..." I say, mortified.

"Shit!" says Emma, helpfully.

"EMMA SAID A BAD WORD!" says Lottie.

I vaguely see Sadie approaching with a horrified look on her face, but the shock of having just *spit coffee onto my boss*—together with my acute awareness that the girls just referred to me as "Mommy" in front of Greyson, who I very explicitly told I did not have kids—seems to have caused my brain to reboot into autopilot mode. I fly out of my seat, grabbing a napkin on the way, and maneuver around Lottie and Emma until I'm standing right beside Greyson. Mumbling an unintelligible apology, I start dabbing at the coffee dripping from his chin, and then—without even thinking about it, and because I've spent the last three years looking after small children every day—I *lift the napkin to my mouth and wet it.*

Greyson looks momentarily horrified as the spit-wetted napkin moves toward his five-o-clock shadow, but—mercifully—he's saved at the very last second by the hand of my sister-in-law closing firmly around my wrist. Thank God for Sadie.

"I'm so sorry," she says when I turn to look at her. The expression on her face looks like she's pleading for forgiveness. She knows I told Greyson I don't have kids, and that I was worried he wouldn't hire me otherwise. "I thought you finished at noon."

"I did," I say. I want to scream. And cry. And laugh. I didn't tell Sadie I was going to have lunch with Greyson. I don't know why. It just felt nice to keep it just for myself. "But we were staying for—"

"The girls—we just came in for cookies—"

"COOKIES?!"

The voice sounds familiar, but it's higher and more animated than I'm used to. I look down, and what I see almost makes me do another spit-take. Greyson is talking to the girls, a comically exaggerated, wide-eyed look of surprise on his face, and both of them are giggling delightedly at him.

"Cookies for *me?*" he says, pointing at himself as though the prospect of cookies is almost too much to bear. "Deeelicious!"

"No, silly!" Lottie laughs. "For us! Bet makes the best cookies in the whole world!"

Greyson nods solemnly. "I bet she does. She makes the best brunch, too. It's so good we even got an extra one!" he says, pointing to the forlorn third plate on the table.

Sadie's grip relaxes on my wrist, but she gives it a gentle tug to get my attention. When I glance at her she shoots me a questioning look and nods towards Greyson.

"Oh, Sadie," I say, somehow recovering a semblance of composure. "This is Greyson Blair, the owner of the mansion up on Old Green Road. Greyson, this is Sadie. My sister-in-law."

Greyson gets to his feet, and Sadie releases my hand to take his.

"A pleasure," he says, giving her a polite nod.

"Likewise," says Sadie, grinning. I can already tell that the Greyson she is meeting, this man who can happily make conversation with small children about cookies, does not mesh with the image she's drawn in her own mind. Frankly, I'm right there with her.

"We'd better get our cookies, girls," says Sadie.

"Bye mister!" says Lottie.

"Bye mister!" copies Emma.

"Bye, little cookie monsters," says Greyson. "Don't forget to ask for extra chocolate chips!"

He grins at them. It's the first time I've seen him smile, and it's just the most spellbinding thing I've seen in a long, long time. He has a knockout smile. The kind of smile that makes nuns rethink their vows.

"Bye, Mommy," says Lottie, grabbing around me. Emma joins in, and all my concern about what Greyson might think melts away as I lean down and pull them both into a tight hug.

"Bye, you two. Be good for your Aunt Sadie and I'll see you later," I say.

Sadie gives me one last apologetic smile, then turns away to herd the girls towards the counter.

I take my seat again, my heart thundering in my chest as the reality of what just happened sinks in. When I glance across at Greyson, he's looking at me with his head slightly tilted and his arms folded across his chest… and a droplet of coffee still clinging to his cheek.

"Uh… you have a little…" I say, pointing to my own cheek.

Greyson picks up a napkin from the table and dabs at his face.

"So," he says, his expression completely straight as he moves his hand down and starts dabbing at the dark spots of coffee on his sweater. "Mommy, huh?"

CHAPTER 6

Greyson

"Yeah, uh..." says Allie, stuttering into silence as she drops her gaze to the table and fiddles nervously with her cup.

I sit across from her, a coffee-stained napkin in my hand, watching her cheeks grow redder and redder. I can't help but notice that she looks good with a flush on her face.

"Thing is..." she says, taking a deep breath and sighing it out.

"BYE, MOMMY!"

Allie spins around in her seat at the sound of the smaller girl's voice. She's by the door with her big sister and their minder, cookies in hand, and they're all waving madly. Allie forces the awkwardness of our conversation off her face as she waves back.

"Bye girls, bye Sadie!"

"Bye Mister!" the bigger girl calls to me.

"Bye, little cookie monsters! Enjoy your feast!"

Their aunt pushes open the door and herds them out. As soon as they're gone, the smile fades from Allie's face as she turns back towards me. I hate the way she's avoiding my gaze. I hate how embarrassed she's clearly feeling. But I'm also more annoyed than I expected to be—more annoyed than I have any right to be.

"Allie," I say, trying to keep my voice even. "Why did you tell me you don't have kids?"

"Well I don't," she says.

I raise a brow at her and watch as she takes a deep breath. Some spirit of determination seems to possess her, and she squares her shoulders and looks up, finally meeting my eye.

"I mean, obviously I do. They're my sister's. Were my sister's. I adopted them a few years ago."

The littlest one can't be much older than three, and all manner of possibilities run through my head. Is her sister a drug addict? Did she run away? Did she die? How the hell does Allie cope? It belatedly occurs to me that it's none of my business, so I maintain an impassive expression and nod.

"Okay, but why didn't you tell me about them?" I ask. "When I asked."

I can feel a bubbling irritation in my gut and I have no idea where it's coming from.

"Because I thought you wouldn't give me the job," she says, in a tone that suggests that it should be the most obvious thing in the world. "And I need it."

And there it is. The source of my irritation. I have somehow managed to convince this beautiful, funny, generous woman that I'm the sort of asshole who wouldn't give a job to a single mother. And I fucking hate it.

And then I realize that I don't actually know if she's single at all.

"So when I asked about you having a husband…" I trail off. I'm pushing it and I know I am. I'm taking advantage of how bad she obviously feels, and I hate myself for it. But I have to know.

"I don't," she says, shaking her head. "It's just me and the girls."

My jaw is tightly clenched. I don't have a clue how to convince her that I'm not the asshole she thinks I am without pulling down the carefully-constructed walls I've been building since I realized that I like her. A lot.

So I drain what's left of my coffee, set it down, and stand up.

"Come on," I say, dropping a few bills on the table and pulling on my coat. "Let's get started."

When she looks up at me, her green eyes are wide with shock.

"You're not firing me?" she asks, her voice wavering.

The question, and the tremble in her voice, hit me like a punch in the gut. I told myself I'd keep her at a distance, that I'd just have to let her think whatever she wants about me, but this… this is too much.

"Nah," I say, trying to stay nonchalant, and hoping it'll help her recover more quickly from whatever emotion is playing out on her pretty face. "I have a policy of never firing people who've spit coffee on me. Too erratic. You never know what they'll do."

The brittle vulnerability on her face clears like clouds after a storm, and her smile is a sunrise breaking through. She stands up quickly, grabs her coat, and roots around in her bag. She pulls out her purse, opens it, and throws down exactly the same amount of money I already left on the table. It's easily more than double what our lunch cost, and I can't help a smile creeping onto my face at just how stubborn she is. I turn around quickly and head outside to avoid her seeing it.

"Thank God for that," she says, tugging her coat closed and doing up her buttons as she catches up to me. "I don't think I could have taken being fired twice in one day."

I stop dead, and she must have still been distracted by her buttons because she walks right into my back. I have to spin around quickly and grab her arms to stop her from falling.

I did have a question, but as I stand there looking down at her, my hands planted on her upper arms, it completely slips my mind.

Maybe, I think, as I watch her slowly blink up at me, maybe the walls could be just a little lower. I glance down at her lips, slightly ajar and pursed in a look of surprise, and wonder if maybe I might be able to add a gate, and open it a little every now and then so she could come inside. I take a breath, and I could swear I'm about to say something foolish, when the moment is suddenly broken by the sound of a loud banging on the diner window.

Sam is standing inside, holding up Allie's Care Bear hat, mouthing "You forgot this!"

My breath comes out as a nervous laugh instead, joining hers, and tinkles all around us like the fragile shards of our almost-kiss.

As she goes inside to retrieve it, I take a moment to clear my head. Stupid. It was a stupid, reckless moment. I avoid relationships at the best of times. Allie is beautiful, smart, and funny… and she has two young children to care for. The least I can do is keep my distance and avoid complicating her life even more.

"So you got fired from the bar, I presume?" I ask when she's back. I speak casually, a little more stiffly than before, but she seems relieved by it. I shove my hands in my pockets and keep a couple of steps away from her as we head around the corner to the parking lot.

"Yup!" she says, matter-of-factly. "Jimmy called me this morning before I started in the diner. JJ—that's his son—is back in town and he needs a job." She shrugs. "That's just how things work around here, you know?"

I don't know, but I nod anyway, fishing the key out of my pocket and hitting the button to unlock the car. It's pristine inside, and still has that new-car smell that somehow lingers in rentals despite the 200,000 miles a year they run.

"I don't mind," she says, pulling on her belt. "JJ is a nice guy. And I was getting pretty tired between all the shifts."

I feel a snake of guilt slither up behind my sternum. I had no way of knowing she was working three jobs so she could support her two children. I guess I just assumed she was saving up for some big vacation, or a house, or something. I feel bad for her, but I get the distinct impression she'd hate that. So I keep my face in check, and simply nod an acknowledgment

Even so, the knowledge that she's now even more dependent on what she earns through HelpForHire cements my resolve to stick around. At least until Christmas. I can find things for her to do, even if I have to invent them.

"You'll have to tell me where to go," I say, pulling out of the lot. "Where first?"

"Left," she says. "And then a right."

Before I even get onto the road she's fiddling with the radio. It never occurs to me to change the radio when I pick up a rental; if there's nothing I like on the stations that came with the car, I just switch to my phone instead. But Allie looks like she's on a mission, sending the radio crackling through static until it picks up on a station, then crinkling her nose adorably before moving on. There's a surprising selection considering where we are.

She stops when she hears a couple of notes of Bon Jovi's Living on a Prayer and gives a little gasp, turning slowly towards me as her eyes widen and her mouth opens with mock-exaggerated delight.

"Are you a fan?"

She shout-sings the first line, by way of response.

"Isn't this from like two decades before you were born?"

Grinning from ear-to-ear, she ignores me and keeps singing at the top of her lungs.

We hit a long straight, and when I glance over again she's playing air guitar along with the instrumental section. I can't help but laugh, and she grins back at me, breaking my heart open a crack.

If you can't beat them, join them. When Bon Jovi kicks back in, I shout-sing right along with Allie. She shoots me an over-the-top wide-eyed look of surprise, then curls her mouth downwards and nods a few times as if to say "not bad, newbie, not bad." We sing our way down the road until she finally directs me through an open double gate to a house with a big yard and a side-alley.

"Kane Warren," Allie says, her face flushed from singing as Bon Jovi's voice fades away. "Electrician. He'll quote you double what he wants so make sure you haggle."

I grin, feeling lighter than I have in a long time, and jump out of the car with her.

※

Every tradesman we meet for the rest of the day over-quotes, and Allie's information about how much they tend to over-quote is invaluable. As is her presence. It couldn't be clearer that every single person we visit is delighted to see her, whether it's the tradespeople or their spouses, and her being there puts us on a more equal footing than if I'd done this alone. All of them are wary of being taken for a ride by the out-of-town city boy.

By dinner time, I have quotes and provisional starting dates for every job I need, except one.

"Shame about Caleb," says Allie from the passenger seat.

Caleb is the plumber. He's out of town visiting his sick mother and his wife has no clue when he'll be back.

"Yeah," I say, without really meaning it. Don't get me wrong, it's a shame his mother is sick. But I feel a little pleased about the delay. It's an excuse to stick around longer.

I pull up back where we started, just up the street from the diner. Allie's car is parked opposite us on the other side of the road.

"Okay," she says, gathering up her stuff. It's amazing how she seems to have turned the passenger side of the car into a nest in only a few hours, using only the things she already had in her bag. There's lip balm on the dash, a half pack of gum in the door, a notepad on the floor beside her feet, a half-empty bottle of water in the cup holder... I'm surprised she didn't have a couple of throw pillows in there. She shoves it all back into her bag and pushes the door open. "See you Friday?"

"See you Friday," I say, barely looking at her.

I don't want her to go. I want her to come back to the mansion with me. I want her to turn half of my couch into her nest, the same way she did with the car. I want half of my bed to be hers.

"Great," she says. "I'll let you know if Caleb calls."

"Au revoir!" I smirk.

She closes the door, pokes her tongue out at me through the window, and waves. The wide grin is still on my face when I pull into the mansion ten minutes later.

CHAPTER 7

Allie

I finish my Friday morning shift at the diner just in time to pick up Emma from preschool and drop her off with Sadie. Just like every day since I got the job at the mansion, she'll collect Lottie from school and look after them until I get off this evening.

Once I've waved them off I sit in my car looking through my playlist to decide what to listen to on the drive. Just as I settle on Lenka's *Everything at Once*, an email notification pops up from HelpForHire.

```
Allie,
```

. . .

```
Could you grab a wrench at the hardware
store on your way over? Will pay you for it
when you get here.


Thanks,


G
```

I stare at it for a while, particularly at the way he's signed off. "G." It's definitely more casual than the "G. Blair" that left me expecting a middle-aged woman, right? And "Thanks" instead of the more formal "Regards". Not to mention that I seem to have graduated from "Ms. Brooks" to just "Allie." Maybe I wasn't hallucinating when I imagined he was about to kiss me outside the diner the other day.

I look up, right into the mirror on the driver's side visor. There's a puzzled frown plastered across my face, and it suddenly strikes me that I'm being ridiculous. I roll my eyes, quickly chastise myself for overanalyzing every part of the message, and put the car into drive.

I arrive at the mansion just after 1 pm, wrench in hand, and let myself in. Greyson is in the kitchen. He's looking casual in jeans, sneakers, and a long-sleeved t-shirt, and he's finishing off a sandwich with his earpods in, watching some sort of video on his laptop.

I can barely take my eyes off the way the white cotton-blend clings to his rippling chest. The bulky sweaters and coats have been hiding multitudes. He's broader and more defined than I'd realized, and it's doing things to me.

"Oh, hey," he says, noticing me. He pulls out a pod and his lips even lift into a half-smile.

"Hey," I say, lifting up the wrench. "Here ya go."

I close the space between us and set the wrench down on the counter, then nod towards the laptop.

"What's that?"

"Plumber," he says, around a mouthful of half-masticated sandwich, and points at the screen. He swallows and turns the laptop to face me a little more, and changes a setting so the sound comes through for me to hear.

"Okaaay," I say, glancing from the screen to Greyson and back again.

"Well," he says. "Caleb is out of town. I have a tap out back that needs fixing. I figured... how hard can it be?"

I lift both my brows at him. He really doesn't seem the type to just... have a go at things. But there's something a bit different about him today. He seems a bit more... open.

"Well..." I say, carefully, watching him pick up the wrench and weigh it in his hand like he's held one before. I'm pretty sure he hasn't. "It could be *pretty* hard, considering Caleb apprenticed with his dad for about ten years before he took over the busin—"

"Psh!" he cuts me off. He's so upbeat I'm stunned into silence. He has an energy about him that I haven't seen before, and it suits him. "If you're that concerned, you can help me."

"Me," I say. I meant it as a question but it comes out as a sort of incredulous, deadpan statement.

"You," he says, nodding. "I just need to finish the video and then we'll head out and have a go at it."

I look at him skeptically but he just turns back to the screen, so I set my bag down and go stand beside him. I guess "small repairs" *was* part of the job description. No sooner have I started watching the video than the on-screen plumber turns a tap and water comes gushing out. I've apparently missed all the actual instructions. This does little to quell my skepticism.

"Which tap is it?" I ask.

"It's way down at the end of the yard," he says, standing. "Out back, beside the old stone shed."

I've never noticed it, so I shrug-nod. "All right. Are you done with your lunch?"

On the table, beside his laptop, I notice that his notepad is covered in coffee rings. Coffee is beginning to feel like the theme of our relationship, between the spilling coffee and the spitting coffee and coffee rings on books. Maybe I should just stop drinking coffee around him. It's not so necessary anymore, anyway; my coffee consumption has dropped by half since Jimmy fired me.

Greyson wipes his hands down on his pants, grabs up the wrench and a toolbox that's so rusted it looks designer, and heads outside. I follow behind him. I'm still pretty skeptical about this whole plan, but either way, I have a feeling that it's going to be an interesting afternoon.

※

"How are the girls?" he asks, as we tromp across the uneven grass.

"Uh," I say, thrown off by the question. "They're good. I had a full day off yesterday so we made forts when they were done with school and watched dinosaurs."

"Dinosaurs, huh?" he asks. I'm surprised by how conversational he is. And intrigued. What's changed?

"Yeah, they love dinosaurs."

"Doesn't everyone?" he smiles, coming to a halt beside the tap.

"I guess so," I say. I hesitate before I go on. Smalltalk usually comes easily to me having grown up in Sunrise Valley, but I always seem to second-guess myself around Greyson. "Do you have kids?"

"Me?" he asks, looking up at me from where he's crouched down, riffling through the toolbox. He shakes his head. "Nope. But my brother has two. A girl and a boy. Four and seven."

"Oh!" I say, eased somewhat by his amiable expression. "Emma and Lottie and three and six. Do you see them much?"

He nods. "My brother is my business partner and he lives just down the street from me. I usually go over there for dinner a couple of times a week."

"You must be missing them," I say, trying to imagine being away from Eddie and Sadie for any length of time. I've been out on my own before, but now, having the girls, family feels so much more important.

He pauses and looks up again, this time with a screwdriver in hand. He tilts his head thoughtfully and then nods.

"Yes," he acknowledges, as though he hasn't really thought about it until now. "Though not as much as I'd have expected to. I'll see them for Thanksgiving. And they're planning a visit next month."

"Here?" I ask, more quickly than I intended.

"Yes."

"You'll still be here next month?"

He looks back down at the tools, and there's a pause before he answers.

"Until Christmas at least," he says. "Though I may have to head back to the city for the occasional meeting."

"But not to see your wife?" I ask, and immediately bite my lower lip. He looks up again, studies me, then gets to his feet and turns toward the tap. I swear I see a hint of a smile creep onto his face as he turns.

"Not to see my wife," he says. "Nor my non-existent girlfriend. Pass me that cloth there, please."

I feel lighter, all of a sudden, and I dutifully lean over to the toolbox and grab out the cloth that's sitting on top, handing it over.

"So you're in marketing and your brother is your business partner," I say, watching him wipe around the old tap with the cloth, clearing away the mud and slimy old leaves that have clung to it. "So you're a city CEO?" I ask.

He snorts a quick laugh. I guess it is a bit of a smalltown-stereotype way to phrase it.

"Get you, Nancy Drew. Yes. And my brother is CTO."

I purse my lips and give an impressed whistle, and he rolls his eyes—but he's grinning.

❄

After about half an hour, I'm prepared to definitively say that he didn't pay enough attention when he was watching the video. That, or plumbing actually is "that hard." He's been straining and pulling at the wrench for a good twenty minutes, and the nut it's secured around has not budged one single bit.

For my contribution, I've stood here watching his forearms tense and the muscles in his back bulge, and his face contort into a grimace every time he tries.

"I'll try some grease," he says, after the three-hundredth attempt. He's nothing if not persistent, I'll give him that.

While he walks over to the toolbox, I tilt my head to look at the tap. The wrench is still attached. In a moment of impulse, I brace my back against the shed, lift my right foot, and give the wrench a little nudge.

Greyson turns around and smirks when he sees what I'm doing.

"It's no good," he says. "It won't budge. I tried ever—"

He cuts off when I kick the wrench again, harder this time. Not because he's annoyed that I tried, but because it actually moved.

There's a brief clang and a rattle, the tap shakes a bit, and the last thing I see is Greyson's shocked face before a strong, powerful jet of clear water shoots out of a gap in the pipe and hits him square in the chest.

"FUCK!"

"OH MY GOD!" I shout, at the same time.

He jumps out of the way, much too late for it to do any good, and he's standing there, staring at me, his hair flattened and dripping, his t-shirt clinging to his muscle-bound torso, drenched from head to toe.

I can't help it. A roll of laughter rumbles up from my belly and out of my mouth. The tap is still spewing water, but I am absolutely weakened by laughter, doubled over, and barely capable of breathing, let alone turning it off.

"Oh, you think that's funny, do you?" he says with a wicked grin, and starts striding towards me.

Before I realize what's happening, Greyson is on me. He grabs around me, pulling me into him, and smushes my face into his sopping wet chest.

"No! Arrgh! Christ, you're soaking!" I cry, still laughing as I wriggle out of his grip and immediately slip on the newly-wet mud, landing square on my backside. "Ow!"

There is a delightful sound ringing in my ears, deep and rich and beautiful, and I realize that it's him, laughing.

He gets down on his knees and takes hold of my calves, pulling me toward him across the mud, and lays into my ribs, tickling me as I squirm and laugh and struggle to catch a breath.

"Stop!" I shout. "Mercy! Mercy! I'm sorry!"

He stops as soon as the words are out of my mouth and props himself up over me on one hand, both of us sputtering out the tail end of our laughter.

"You're soaked!" I say, between chuckles.

"Thanks to you," he accuses.

His smile fades and he looms over me, looking down with the same intensity he had outside the diner. This time, there is no Sam to knock on the window and distract us. There is just him, and me, and the crackling, electrified air between us. He pushes a curl out of my face and suddenly, but not without welcome, his lips are on mine.

I'm laying in the cold, wet mud, soaked through to the skin, but my body feels suddenly hot all over. His hand is on my cheek, his weight pressed against me but restrained, and his lips are surprisingly soft. I reach up, entangle my muddy fingers into his soaking wet hair and pull him deeper. He rumbles a groan into my mouth and I match it with a soft moan, as my hips involuntarily lift off the hard ground towards him.

When he finally pulls back, I honestly don't know how long it's been. I press my teeth into my bottom lip and clear my throat. He pushes himself up and stands, then reaches down for my hand.

I smile at him as he pulls me up, and the corners of his mouth tug upward a little. But once I'm on my feet, he lets go of my hand and reclaims some distance, yanking on the wrench to stop the flow of water. He looks back over to me, and his face is unreadable. He looks embarrassed, or maybe annoyed, and there is no smile in his eyes. My heart stops somersaulting and flops to a standstill.

When the hissing of the tap subsides, I feel weirdly awkward in the silence. And it doesn't seem like Greyson is inclined to break it.

"We'd better change," I say, desperate to fill the void. "Or we'll get sick."

He drops the wrench into the toolbox with a clang and picks the box up by its handles.

"I don't get sick," he says as he turns back towards the house. I trail behind, lost in confusion about what the hell just happened between us.

CHAPTER 8

Greyson

I'm sick.

It's been three days since Allie was here, two days since the first sneeze, and about 20 hours since the last time I got up from the couch to do anything but pee or fetch more water. The grand old reception room is littered with used tissues and empty plastic bottles. One minute I'm burning up, the next there aren't enough blankets in the world to keep me warm, and I keep dozing off. Every muscle in my body aches, my throat is full of thorns, and my laptop ran out of battery hours ago but I can't muster the strength to go upstairs and fetch my charger. So I'm just lying here in the silence, listening to the way the old house creaks with the wind, waiting to feel less shitty.

It wouldn't be so bad, but every time I wake up I end up thinking back to the last time Allie was here, when, in a moment of abject stupidity, I kissed her. And then I groan. And then my throat hurts. It's a vicious cycle.

Why did I do it? I know why. And the fever I'm running has made it impossible to engage in the kind of mental gymnastics I'd ordinarily use to push the thought out of my brain.

It's because I like her. And because it bothered me that my efforts to keep her at arms' length had made her think I was a less-charismatic version of Mr. Burns from The Simpsons. Sitting in my dark, oak-lined office, fingers steepled, cackling as I shredded the resumes of single mothers. It pissed me off. So I figured, what's the harm in just being nice?

Well, now we know. When you're nice to beautiful, funny, kind, stubborn, slightly eccentric women named Allie, they do things like smile at you and laugh with you, and they swirl you up in the vortex of who they are until you find yourself laying in a puddle of mud, kissing them.

Now don't get me wrong. It's not the kiss that bothers me. It was the best kiss I've ever had, bar none. Her lips were soft and pliable, her breath was warm against my winter-chilled skin, and having her underneath me was just about the most perfect feeling I've ever known.

No, what makes me cringe is the memory of what happened afterward, when I came back to the house, gave awkward, one-word replies to all her attempts at conversation, probably made her feel like crap, and then pretended I had meetings for the rest of the day so I could disappear into my bedroom like some sullen teenager.

Well played, Greyson. Real mature.

I groan out loud again at the memory of it, and then I cough so hard I'm surprised I don't hack up half a lung right onto old Aunt Julia's antique quilt.

I start to doze off again, the memories still swirling in my fevered brain. My eyes jolt open like I've been hit with a surge of adrenaline, and I find myself standing in some kind of dark, frost-laden hedge maze. The freezing air burns my throat as I breathe, and Allie is here. Her little girls are, too. They're running away from her, their laughter echoing through the night. They think they're playing hide-and-seek, but Allie is chasing after them, frantic. I'm trying to catch up to her, but every time I round a corner I only catch a glimpse of her as she rounds the next one. No matter how fast I run, no matter how hard my heart pumps or how much my thighs burn, I can't reach her.

"Allie!" I shout, desperately. She turns around and smiles at me, and the hedges all around us suddenly burst into flame. I run to her through the scorching hot corridor of burning trees, wrapping my arms around her and squeezing her tight.

"You're sick!" she hisses beside my ear.

"Allie…" I say, but I don't know how to reply. She looks so disgusted with me, so angry.

"You're sick!" she spits again, and when I try to hold her a little tighter, she begins to crumble. Her face cracks—literally—and she begins to turn into dust. I desperately try to hold onto her, but the harder I try the more I break her, and the hot wind whips the dust up and away, and the girls are suddenly there beside me, screaming for their mommy.

"ALLIE!" I scream, and the dream breaks.

I'm sitting on the couch with cold sweat clinging to my forehead and my heart stampeding around my chest like a bull at a rodeo. My lungs are forcing great, gulping breaths in and out of me in an effort to calm it down. It takes my eyes a moment to adjust to the room's dim light before I notice a silhouette on the other side of the coffee table.

There's a long pause as I try to work out whether this is still part of the dream or a trick of the light. But then the silhouette shifts slightly and speaks to me in a familiar voice.

"Yes?"

It's Allie. Not a cloud of dust in a burning maze, but standing in the reception room of Sunrise Valley House.

Shit. I must have shouted her name out loud. And now I'm sitting here rapidly mouth-breathing at her like a complete lunatic.

"Er—nothing," I say quickly and lay back down, trying to get my breathing under control.

A coughing fit takes me, and before I even realize she's moved around the coffee table, Allie's cool fingers rest gently on my forehead.

"You're sick," she says.

She's looking down at me with her brows drawn in concern, and it creases a small, vertical line just above the bridge of her nose. She looks like an angel. A frowny angel.

"I tried to call but there was no answer."

"I was sleeping," I tell her.

She removes her fingers, and I immediately miss her touch. A moment later there's a loud SHHH sound as she pulls the curtains open and the bright sunlight of a crisp winter's afternoon floods in to burn my eyes out of their sockets.

"AARGH! What the f…"

I blink and squint, and once my eyes have adjusted to the light I see her looking around the room at all the tissues and bottles I've accumulated. It seems like my being sick is a distraction from whatever awkwardness there was the other day. Maybe I can just stay sick forever.

"Have you eaten?" she asks, bending to pick up a bottle from the floor.

"Not hungry," I croak. "Leave it. I'll do it lat—"

I cut off as a cough overtakes me, and she comes to my side and slaps me on the back.

"You need to eat," she says. "Got any soup?"

I shake my head no.

She places her hand on my back again and frowns at me.

"You're soaked, Greyson. And the fire is out."

I hadn't realized the fire had gone out. And I like the way she says my name.

"It's fine," I say.

"It's not fine," she insists. "You need to shower or you'll end up with pneumonia or something. Go do that and I'll make the fire again."

I don't want to. I really, really don't want to. But I am sort of damp and it is sort of cold, so I accept her hand and let out a groan as she pulls me up to my feet.

The shower actually does make me feel considerably better. I'm still sick, everything still sucks, but at least it sucks while I'm wearing dry, comfortable clothes that don't have the stench of two days of fever-induced body odor clinging to them.

When I get back into the sitting room it looks completely different. The pile of blankets I've been wallowing under for the last couple of days is gone and there are some fresh blankets neatly folded on the edge of the couch. The bottles and tissues have all disappeared, the couch cushions are fluffed and arranged where they should be, and there's a steaming mug of coffee on the table, with a plate of pop tarts beside it.

"Feeling better?" asks Allie, coming in from the kitchen.

"Yeah," I croak. "Hey, you didn't have to do all this."

She's waving her hand to dismiss me before I've even finished.

"You don't have any food," she says and nods to the plate. "I found those in my bag. They're Lottie's favorite."

"Thanks," I say, managing to lift a smile for her. I sit down and grab the coffee, taking a sip that burns and then soothes my scratched-up throat as it passes. "I was going to get groceries yesterday, but I really didn't feel like going out."

"I hear man flu is the worst kind of flu," she says.

I lift a brow at her. I don't quite manage to pull it off because a cough overtakes me and I have to set the coffee down so I don't spill it.

"I've put the blankets in the machine," says Allie. "And I changed the bedding in the master bedroom. I hope you don't mind."

I shake my head. She's some sort of angel, I'm sure of it, and the more I watch her speak and notice her lips move, the more I'm transported back to the muddy puddle where I tasted them. It was reckless and stupid, but I wish I'd found out where it might have led instead of stalking away like a petulant child.

"Thank you," I say. "For all this. I should have called to cancel today but I forgot you were coming."

She's silent for a moment, and when I look up she glances away.

"No worries," she says, doing up her coat. "I'd better head off to pick up the girls."

I have to fight with myself to resist asking her to stay. It's a good thing I'm in a weakened state or I'd have lost.

"Okay," I say, nodding.

"Okay," she says. She picks up her bag and stands there for a moment, looking a little awkward. Looking like she wants to say something. As desperately as I want to know what it is, I'm terrified of finding out. Because I know that if she'd come to my room that afternoon instead of keeping her distance, I would have taken her to bed. And no amount of mental gymnastics would have saved me. Or her.

"I lit the fire," she says suddenly, and takes off before I can say another word. The fire is roaring and the room is cozy, but it somehow feels colder the second she's gone.

❄

"Greyson? It's me!"

I am roused suddenly from my sleep by the sound of a voice at the front door, and, moments later, the sound of it slamming shut.

"Allie?" I call.

I haven't closed the curtains and I can see that the sky outside is dark. Black and grey with rolling clouds. I pick up my phone with a frown, squint at the brightness of it, and see that it's just after 7 pm.

She appears in the doorway with a smile, and I feel my heart take flight.

"Hey," I say, tilting my head to the side and smiling at her.

"Hey," she says, stepping inside. "How are you feeling?"

"Awake," I answer. I can't wipe the sleepy smile off my face and I see hers grow a little when she notices.

"Sorry. Serves you right for sleeping on the couch all the time," she says. "Beds are for sleeping."

"Sorry, *mom*."

She snorts a laugh as she peels off her coat and drapes it over a chair.

"The girls begged to have a sleepover with Sadie's kids. They're doing princess movie night. So I decided to bring you some groceries and make you some soup." She smiles, holding up a plastic grocery bag.

"That's… really kind," I tell her.

"I'll stay the night on the couch," she says. "Since that's the only way you'll get off it and go to bed."

If only she knew, I think to myself as I watch her trot out to the kitchen, how much more appealing the couch would be with her sleeping on it.

As I lie there, listening to her clank about with pots and pans, looking at the remains of the molten-lava flavor pop tarts that I managed to cram down earlier, a feeling of satisfaction washes over me like a warm blanket. My brain is still on guard, but my heart, or my dick, or maybe both, are very, very happy that Alora Brooks is going to be spending the night at Sunrise Valley House.

"Here we go!" she says, appearing in the doorway twenty minutes later carrying two deep bowls.

I slide over for her to sit down beside me, and lean over the bowl as she places it down in front of me, taking a large sniff of the steam that's coming off it.

"Mmmm," I say.

"You can't smell a damn thing, you rotten liar," she chides with a smile, and I manage a little laugh before the coughing kicks in again.

"I'm sure it smells delicious, anyway," I say.

"It does," she nods. "It's Bet's recipe. And it's good for colds."

"Flu," I correct. "MAN flu."

"If you insist," she says, smiling. "Find something we can watch."

It strikes me as strange that, as I sit on the couch in the throes of possibly the worst virus I've ever had, flicking through a streaming site to find something to watch with the woman I hired to clean and paint, I feel more content than I can remember being in a long, long time.

"Oooh, that one," says Allie, jabbing her spoon toward my screen so enthusiastically I'm forced to lay a protective hand over my keyboard for fear of soup flicks getting between the keys.

"Die Hard?" I say, giving her a skeptical look. She nods enthusiastically.

"It's not even Thanksgiving yet," I say, trying to suppress a smile.

"One," she says, holding up a finger. "Good call. Die Hard is definitely a Christmas movie."

I grin.

"And two," she says, flicking up another finger, "if I have to wear antlers to serve brunch it's not too early for Christmas movies."

I let out a burst of laughter.

"Fair point," I say, and hit play. I settle back on the couch, unable to taste the best soup I've ever had, and feel a wash of happiness settle over me as we watch Bruce Willis touch down in L.A.

CHAPTER 9

Allie

I wake up slowly, rousing from a deep slumber and stretching my arms up over my head. When I finally open my eyes it takes me a second to remember where I am. It's such a strange feeling, having had a full night's sleep without my bed being invaded in the middle of the night by sweet but *very* determined little kick-monsters.

"Penelope Wrinklebottom Foxtrot," I say, because if you *can* change the audio cue that your phone's AI assistant responds to, I can't think of a single reason you wouldn't. "What time is it?"

The robotic voice informs me that it's 8:30 am—an hour later than I've woken up in three years—and I grin to myself as I pull the blanket back up to my chin.

I must have fallen asleep watching the movie last night with Greyson, and he must have draped the blanket over me before going to bed himself. Which is pretty sweet, really. I woke up at about 3 am, changed into my pajamas, stoked the fire back to life, and went back to sleep.

I haven't mentioned the kiss to Greyson since it happened, and he hasn't mentioned it to me. He's either still as mortified as he was that day, when he basically disappeared from sight for the whole afternoon, or he's too sick to tackle the conversation. In which case, I wish man flu upon him forevermore. Frankly, it's pretty rude to kiss a girl like that, shift the whole world underneath her, make her hips thrust themselves towards you so she can't deny where she wanted this to go, and then... disappear.

I grab my phone, have a leisurely browse around my social media feeds just for the novelty of doing anything at a leisurely pace, and then hit dial to call Sadie and check on the kids.

"Ugh! Can you believe it?" she says as soon as she answers the call. There's a clanking noise like she's tidying up the pots and pans in the kitchen, and I can hear the chatter and giggles of the kids distantly in the background.

"I mean, the timing just could *not* be better," she continues, her voice thick with sarcasm. "I was supposed to take Grace to the orthodontist today."

I frown. I knew Sadie's eldest had an appointment this afternoon, but...

"You can't go?" I ask.

The clanking stops abruptly and Sadie levels her voice.

"Allie... haven't you looked outside yet?"

"No," I say, and reluctantly pull the warm blankets off myself. The fire is still glowing, but the wooden floor is cold on my bare feet and my pajama shorts are doing little to ward off the chill.

I pull the curtains open and immediately screw up my eyes as I'm assaulted by a blinding light. I open one eye just a slit, and then both of them, wide.

"Oh," I say.

The ground is blanketed in at least three feet of fluffy white snow, and fat flakes are still floating down from the grey sky. It looks beautiful, but when you grow up in a small town in upstate New York you learn to let go of your love of snow as soon as you're done with school. It gets in the way, and the local officials are seldom of a mind to get it out of the way.

"Shit."

"Yeah," says Sadie. "Well anyway, I guess I'm in all day so no rush to get here. Assuming you can. It looks like it's still coming down pretty heavy."

"Sorry about Grace's appointment," I tell her. "Will you be able to reschedule?"

"Yeah, it sucks," she says. "But I'm sure we'll manage."

"Good. Are the girls all right?"

"They're fine," Sadie says. "They're all getting their snowsuits on so we can go make snow angels and snowmen. Listen."

I assume she holds the phone away from her ear and toward the kids because I can hear them all chattering and squabbling as they get themselves snow-ready. They sound so excited and happy, and I feel a pang of remorse that I'm not there to join in the fun.

"Your brother's in the garage trying to dig out the sleigh," Sadie goes on when the phone is back beside her ear. "Everything's good here. Don't worry, okay?"

I smile to myself. No-one is better at reassurance than Sadie.

"Okay," I say.

"How is Fluface McSickpants?"

"You know he has a name, right?" I ask.

"Yeah. But that's no fun."

"He's alhink," I laugh. "I haven't seen him today yet."

"So he's not... beside you, then?" she asks, and I can hear her grinning.

"Bye Sadie," I reply, trying to make my voice sound like I'm rolling my eyes.

"I just meant that maybe you shared a bed, like a sleepover."

"Oh, *of course* you did."

"Sam said he's hot."

"Your brother thinks anyone from out of town is hot," I laugh.

"Fair point," she says. "Oh, Eddie's got the sleigh. Love you."

"Love you," I say. "And thanks again!"

"No proble—"

She always hangs up mid-word.

Looking back out of the window, I push up onto the tips of my toes to try and see if Old Green Road is passable, but everything is so stark white it's hard to tell the roads from the hedges. I decide to head upstairs and see if one of the higher windows has a better vantage point. I grab my little washup bag so I can brush my teeth and freshen up along the way.

I head into the first room at the top of the stairs, a spare bedroom at the front of the house. I suppose they're all spare rooms except for Greyson's, and even that isn't really in use. When I was in there yesterday to change the bedding, I noticed that he's still living out of his luggage, despite the huge wardrobes and chests dotted around the room. I've been studiously ignoring the pang of sadness I felt at the reminder that his stay here in Sunrise Valley is temporary.

When I get to the window, I have to squint to see Old Green Road at all. It's not looking good. There are no tire tracks, and if you didn't already know it was there, you might not even notice the dip in the snow where the road meets the snow-covered hedges. And it's still coming down.

With my brow furrowed and a thousand sudden worries running through my mind—most of them about the girls—I head for the bathroom. It's not that I don't trust Sadie, because I do—completely. But if they end up having to stay over there again tonight, the likelihood that the snow will have cleared by tomorrow is slim-to-none. It'll be the first time they've spent more than one night away from me since their mother passed, and even though I know they're in good hands it still feels like a big deal.

I enter the huge bathroom, drop my toiletries bag down on the countertop beside the door, and let out a deep sigh as I rub my eyes, willing all the worries out of my mind. It doesn't work. So I sigh again, open my little bag, pull out my toothbrush, and look up into the mirror to brush my teeth.

"HOLY SHIT!" I scream. A shadowy figure is looming over my shoulder in the fogged-up mirror. Instinctively, without a second thought, I spin around on my heels and raise my arms to defend myself.

Greyson is standing there, butt-naked, both hands over his package, staring at me with wide, alarmed eyes.

"OH MY GOD!"

My hand comes up immediately to cover my eyes, but not before I notice that his shoulders really are much broader than I originally thought, and his body is somehow every bit as honed and toned as I imagined it would be. Maybe even a little bit more.

"WHY ARE YOU NAKED?!?" It comes out like an accusation, but in my defense, five seconds ago I was expecting to have to fend off a home invader with a toothbrush.

"I'm *in the bathroom!*" he replies, his tone just as accusatory as mine.

"OKAY, THAT'S a... fair... point." I trail off as I realize that he does, indeed, have some pretty strong arguments on his side of this situation.

"Nice pajamas, by the way," he says, making me glance down.

My shorts are short and covered in blue hearts, and I've paired them with a too-big, cozy fleece top.

"Shut up," I say, secretly pleased that he's looking.

"I bet you say that to all your employers."

I feel the smile crack on my face, and back up toward the door.

"I'll just..." I slap my spare hand around on top of the counter until I find my wash bag, then bump up against the door. "I'll just come back later."

I scrunch my eyes tightly closed and fumble around behind me, trying to find the door handle.

"Bye, then," he says, and I can hear a smile thickening his voice.

"Bye!" I call, my voice a little manic as my hand finally closes around the handle of the door and I pull it open to make my escape.

When I'm halfway down the stairs, I hear Greyson burst out laughing in the bathroom, and it echoes all through the house.

CHAPTER 10

Greyson

The look on Allie's face when she walked into the bathroom and caught me in the buff will stay with me for the rest of my life, I'm sure of it. Even though I know she can hear me, it's a good five minutes before I can stop myself laughing.

When I eventually look back at the mirror to finish washing up, the wide grin on my face takes me by surprise. It's so alien to me. I've spent so long keeping my head down, focusing on work, keeping everyone at arm's length, and avoiding entanglements, that I haven't given myself a reason to laugh in a long, long time. But Allie… she makes me laugh every time I see her.

I finish up, get dressed, and head downstairs to the kitchen. I'm feeling about halfway better today. My fever has broken, my nose has cleared just a bit, and I sound way worse than I did yesterday. "You sound awful—you must be feeling better," my mother used to say when I was a kid.

The house is toasty warm and Allie is in the kitchen, making a coffee. I've noticed that she drinks almost as much coffee as me, and her brews are just as strong. Little wonder where she gets her energy.

She's wearing a bright red sweater and a pair of blue jeans, and her feet are bare on the kitchen rug. There's something about having her barefoot in my house that makes my inner caveman roar.

"Hey," she says, glancing at me. Her cheeks immediately flush and she turns away to pour two mugs.

"Hey," I croak, perching on one of the high stools.

"Oh, you sound worse," she says. "Are you feeling better?"

Wise woman.

"Yeah, I think so."

"Listen, I'm sorry about earlier. I should have knocked."

She turns around and places a mug down on the island, then pushes it across to me. I dip my head a little, staring at her until she's forced to look up and meet my eye.

"I should have put a lock on the door by now," I say. "And besides, I think I'd rather you see me naked than the pathetic state I was in yesterday."

"Me, too," she nods. And then I get to watch her adorable face turn the same color as her sweater as she realizes what she just said.

"I… I mean," she stutters. "I'm glad you're feeling better did you see it snowed?"

The way she rushes on with no discernible pause makes me smirk. I lift my mug and take a sip to hide it, and nod.

"There's no way I'll get home today if the snow keeps coming down. The council never bothers to clear it before it's almost melted away of its own accord."

Her flush begins to fade as her brow draws down with concern. She looks out the nearby window, where the snow is indeed still falling.

"Are the girls all right?"

"They're fine," she says, nodding. "Sadie has them. I called earlier and they were all heading out to make snowmen."

"Sounds like they'll have a blast."

"Yeah," she agrees, giving me a gentle smile. Her shoulders seem to drop slightly—with relief, I think—and I get more satisfaction out of making her feel just a little bit better than I ever have out of making a big business deal.

"Weren't you supposed to fly home later?" she asks.

"Shit!"

She's probably right. It slipped my mind in the craziness of the past few days, but it's almost Thanksgiving and I'm pretty sure today is the day that Ben scheduled my flight back to New York. I pull out my phone to check my reminders and, sure enough, there it is. A 6 pm United flight from Plattsburgh to LaGuardia.

"Shit," I repeat, looking back to the window. "Any idea how long it's supposed to last?"

Allie gives a little shrug.

"It's supposed to stop snowing tonight, but if it's cold enough the snow will freeze hard. Might take a full day of sunshine to clear."

I grunt with irritation and start tapping out an email. Ben is a mastermind at this sort of thing. He'll fix it.

"Did you sleep all right?" I ask, shoving my phone back in my pocket.

"Like a rock," Allie says. "I normally have little feet digging me in the ribs all night. Not that I'd change it."

I smile. I want to ask her how she came to be the sole guardian of the two little girls who call her Mommy, but it seems like that would be prying too much.

"So," she says. "Since I'm stuck here for the day, I'm going to sand the paneling in the back bedroom. And you should concentrate on getting better so you can catch your flight when the snow clears and have a good Thanksgiving with your family."

"Yes, boss," I say, giving her a salute.

She blushes again, and the urge to pull her over the counter and into my lap is almost irresistible. Even in my weakened state, I think I could muster the strength. I'm actually considering it when my phone starts ringing.

I pop it on the counter and hit the speaker button.

"Hey, Ben."

"Hey, Boss," he says, and I can tell instantly that it's not good news.

"Hit me."

"All flights are booked up until the day after Thanksgiving. I checked every airport on both sides. You could drive it, but it's six hours without the snow, and from what you said you can't get out of the town anyway."

"Shit," I say. I glance up and Allie is frowning at me.

"I'll keep trying. Sorry, Boss."

"Not your fault," I tell him. "Do me a favor and let Ethan know. I'm supposed to be with him and Emily for Thanksgiving."

"Will do. Oh, you have an email about the LPF contract," he says. "They're making some noise. If you get a chance."

"All right. Thanks, Ben."

"No worries, G. Get some rest, you sound like shit."

I hear Allie snort a laugh from across the room.

"Thank you, soon-to-be-former assistant."

"You'd be dead in three days without me," he shoots back. He's not wrong.

"Well, let's not put that to the test while I'm stuck in four feet of snow in the middle of nowhere. I'll talk to you later."

"Later," he says, and hangs up.

I let out a deep sigh and rub my temples, then turn apologetically to Allie.

"Sorry, I need to check something for work. I'll only be a minute."

Allie waves her hand at me. "Sure, go ahead! If it takes longer than that, I've got sanding to do anyway." She grins at me.

I flick through my phone and bring up the LPF email that Ben mentioned. LPF stands for Lincoln Peterson Finance, and Lincoln Peterson is the exact type of asshole you'd expect of someone who's one step above a loan shark. He is also, however, the exact type of narcissist that is very keen to maintain his brand image. This means he is willing to pay us large sums of money to make him look good. It also means that he is an absolute nightmare to work with.

He's demanding a meeting with me personally. I can see in the email that Ethan has offered to meet him, but Peterson is having none of it. Despite the fact that Ethan and I co-own the business and have exactly the same amount of clout, Peterson's ego won't let him deal with anyone but the CEO.

I sigh out loud as I close the email and put my phone away, and Allie looks at me with visible concern.

"Everything all right?"

"Yeah," I say. "Awkward client. I'll deal with it tomorrow."

"You know," she says, then hesitates a little before continuing. "The girls and I are going over to Eddie's house—that's my brother, Sadie's husband—for Thanksgiving. Sam will come over for dinner, too. Sam from the diner? He's Sadie's brother. And his boyfriend will be there. I'm sure it would be no trouble to set a place for one more. You know, if you're stuck."

I'm not sure whether I'm surprised more by her generosity or by the fact that literally everyone I've met in the town seems to be going to the same place for Thanksgiving. It's nice, in a way.

"I..." My turn to hesitate.

Do I want to spend Thanksgiving with Allie and her entire clan, eating turkey 'til I look like I swallowed a beach ball?

Hell yes, I do.

And that's the problem. Because the more time I spend with her, the more I feel my resolve weakening. The more I start wondering if I could make it work this time, and the more I forget why I'm so careful never to get too close to anyone.

But here she is, in front of me, looking up at me expectantly—maybe even a little hopefully. What chance do I have against that?

"That's really kind of you," I say after a pause. "If I'm stuck here, I might take you up on it."

She smiles, and I realize she's happy about my answer. Maybe my sullen-teenager act the other day didn't bother her that much after all. Maybe, maybe, maybe... I'm letting myself think that word far too often these past few weeks.

"Oh, hey," she says, "If and when I do get out of here, I won't be back until after Thanksgiving. You were supposed to be out of town, and I always help Bet to prepare a load of food in the diner before Thanksgiving. She puts out a free meal on the day and invites all the older folks along."

"That's... really generous of her," I say. It's starting to seem like an uncommonly common trait in this little town.

"Yeah, it's nice. A lot of them are widows and widowers and their kids moved away years ago. It gives them somewhere to go and have some company."

I don't say anything for a moment. I'm struggling with the idea of being widowed, and I realize it's because for the first time in a very long time I've been imagining being with someone properly. Being with Allie. Maybe forever.

I'm also struck by the fact that I can't remember the last time I did something like that—something generous, something that makes the world a little better, just for its own sake. Allie seems to do nothing else.

"I'll help," I say, before I even realize I've made the decision.

She looks up at me with her brows lifted, surprise and delight clear on her face.

"Really?"

"Yeah," I nod. "If I'm stuck here, I might as well, right?"

Now I'm actually looking forward to helping Allie peel carrots in the diner. What is wrong with me?

"Okay," she grins, nodding. "I'll let Bet know. Thanks!"

She almost skips out of the room, leaving me sitting there in a warm glow to finish my luke-warm coffee.

❄

The house is a sturdy old build. For the last few hours, I've been laying on the couch, resting, streaming some shows I've never heard of, and listening to the quiet hum of the sander from upstairs.

I never chill like this back home; I'm always too busy. I am admittedly still not feeling great, though. The fatigue is pretty debilitating and my bones ache when I move. But I still feel guilty for sitting here doing nothing while Allie is upstairs working.

I push myself up from the couch with a groan and head into the kitchen, intent on making Allie a coffee. But as I pass by the chair in the hallway, distracted by a thud from upstairs, I accidentally knock her bag off the seat and send its contents scattering across the floor.

"Shit!"

I bend down and start cleaning up the mess. Mostly, they're things you'd expect the mother of two girls to be carrying; baby wipes, a purse, a lollipop, lip balm. There's also a dinosaur card game, which brings a smile to my face.

But then, as I get down on all fours to make sure I've got everything, I notice a stack of papers lying just behind the chair. They must have skitted under it after falling out of the bag. As I pick them up, I realize they're drawings. And they're enchanting.

The first one is a sketch of two little girls, standing beside a car as a woman with a mop of curly hair tries to yank open a car door. There's a speech bubble coming from the woman that says "Shit!", another from the littlest girl, that also says "Shit!", and another from the bigger girl that says "That's a bad word!"

The cartoons are fairly simple, in some ways, but the shading on them draws me in. There is real light and personality in the faces, and if I were looking at these as part of a portfolio for our art department, I'd be impressed.

I leaf through the others, half-aware that I'm snooping, but every single one brings a smile to my face. They're all relatable slices of life drawn with love, and I can't believe this woman, who already has so much going for her, is this talented a cartoonist as well. She's beautiful, kind, funny, generous, and… artistic. She's too good to be true.

Smiling, and feeling grateful for this new glimpse of Allie's world that I hadn't seen before, I push the papers back into the bag and head into the kitchen. A coffee really seems like the least I can do to make up for my snooping.

❄

I had planned to knock on the door, but Allie has left it half-open. I push it with my free hand, and as it swings open I have to stifle a laugh at the scene that lies before me. The panels on the wall are almost finished, and Allie is taking a break. By which I mean, she's wearing a pair of huge pink headphones and dancing around with the sander whirring away in her hand. I mean, she's really going for it.

"If you like being a banana!" she shout-sings. "And getting caught in the rain!"

I feel my lips twitch and my mouth pinches into a pucker as I desperately try not to laugh. I lean against the door jamb and just watch her. What she lacks in rhythm, she more than makes up for in enthusiasm. Her little hips swing wildly as she twirls about, leaving streaks in the sawdust around her feet.

And then, after a particularly energetic pirouette, she notices me.

"OH!"

She stops dead in her tracks and bites her bottom lip, a slight flush reddening her cheeks. She clicks a little button on the sander to turn it off and pulls her headphones down around her neck. I can hear the tinny notes of *The Pina Colada Song* coming out of them as she stands there, breathing just hard enough for it to sound… appealing.

I should tease her. I really should. But I'm concentrating too hard on not popping the world's most awkward boner.

"Hey!" she says.

"Hey," I say, holding out the coffee. "I brought you this."

"You're supposed to be resting," she says, coming over to take it. "But thanks."

"I felt bad," I admit. "I'm down there flicking through Netflix and you're up here working hard."

She shrugs. "I have my music. It's all good."

We smile at each other as we sip our coffee. I decide, having won the battle against my boner for now, that it's about time to tease her.

"You know... it's Pina Colada."

She looks at me with a confused frown.

I bob my head back and forth and sing: "If you like Pina Coladas, and getting caught in the rain..."

Slowly, as she realizes what I'm talking about, her left eyebrow raises into a high arch and her lips tug upwards into a tight, barely restrained smile.

"REEEEEALLY?"

Her voice is laden with sarcasm, and I get the distinct impression that my teasing is about to bite me in the ass.

"Do you mean to tell me," she continues, clearly relishing the trap that I have apparently fallen into, "that all this time, The Pina Colada song has been about... Pina Coladas? Why was I not informed? Was there a memo at some point?"

"All right, I see this isn't going to work out well for me," I try to interject, but she's on a roll.

"Please Mr. Big City, lend me your worldly wisdom! For I am but a humble small-town girl, who wouldn't know a Pina Colada from a Cosmopolitan from a hole in the ground!"

"ALL RIGHT, I give in!"

Her face breaks into a wide smile, and I find myself grinning back at her. Then her smile softens, and a faraway expression paints itself across her face.

"It might be The Pina Colada Song to you and me. But when Emma sings it, it's a song about being a banana in the rain."

Now. Now, at this moment, I want to kiss her more than I've ever wanted to do anything in my whole life. And this morning in the kitchen, I wanted to kiss her more than I've ever wanted to do anything in my whole life. She is rapidly taking up all the spots in my top ten list of things I want to do more than anything I've ever done in my whole life.

I smile back at her, but the effect she has on me makes my chest tighten with panic. What am I doing? And why do I seem so unable to stop myself from doing it? We've reached the point where I'm spending Thanksgiving with her family and we're doing charity events together. What's happening to me?

"I was just going to finish up and start dinner," she says, just like that, as though she and I having dinner together is the most normal and unremarkable thing in the world.

"Sounds great!" I say, and turn towards the door. "See you soon, then."

I don't wait for her reply before I head back down the stairs. I feel caged by my own desire for her, and every second we spend together feels like a point of no return.

We're approaching a precipice. I can feel it, and I'm not sure I have the willpower to stop myself from jumping.

CHAPTER 11

Allie

It's the third day of the snow-in and I'm starting to feel antsy. It's not that I don't enjoy Greyson's company—he's actually pretty fun when he's not being weird and standoffish. But I miss the girls, and every time I sleep until I'm rested or finishing a coffee before it gets stone cold, I feel guilty for enjoying it.

At least Greyson is feeling better. He's practically bouncing around the house today. I think he has that post-viral glow you get when you were sick enough for long enough to forget what normal feels like, so for a day or two afterward, normal feels like you have superpowers because you can make a sandwich without needing to go lie down halfway through.

"Here we go!" he says, gliding into the sitting room with a plate in each hand. He sets them down on the table in front of me. Grilled cheese sandwiches. Man, he's such a bachelor.

"Thanks." I smile, but I know it doesn't quite reach my eyes. I've called Sadie and spoken to the girls a bunch of times over the past couple of days, and everything really is fine, but being away from them is just starting to sit uneasily with me.

"No problem," says Greyson. "You're not allowed to lift a finger today. I need to pay you back for caring for me when I was all sick and weak. And naked."

"There's no need," I grin. I mean it. I keep having happy little flashbacks to our encounter in the bathroom, and I'm more than willing to call us even.

"Yes, there is," he insists, biting off a chunk of his sandwich. He chews and swallows. "I need to prove my manliness. This is how masculinity works. Later on, I'm going to make you watch me lift something heavy for no reason."

I laugh, shaking my head. When he's not very obviously avoiding me, he's really nice to be around. And the fact that he looks like an underwear model doesn't hurt.

I lift up the sandwich and take a bite, and my entire mouth explodes with flavor.

"Oh my god!" I say around my mouthful, looking over to him. I chew and chew until I can swallow. "What the hell is in this? It's divine."

His face morphs into a smug grin.

"Right? I wish I could take credit, but it's Ethan's invention. Worcestershire sauce, mayo, and super-fine diced pickle."

"It's amaaaaazing," I coo, taking another bite. Just as I'm wondering how I can get Greyson to make me gourmet bachelor food more often, his phone starts ringing on the table, and he slides it towards himself to look at the screen.

"Ha! Speak of the devil," says Greyson, pressing the speaker button. "Hey, Bro."

It's almost disconcerting, how completely at-ease he is with me listening in to his conversations.

"Hey, G!"

The man on the other end has a similar voice to Greyson. Maybe a little higher in pitch, and a little friendlier.

"Shame about being snowed in the ass-end of bumfuck nowhere." Ethan chuckles, and Greyson gives me an apologetic smile.

"Hey!" I say.

"Oh no! A native!" says Ethan, and I like him immediately. "Is that Allie?"

I glance at Greyson with raised brows. His brother knows my name? What else does he know about me?

Greyson keeps his gaze studiously on the phone.

"Yeah. She's snowed in here with me."

"Ohhh," says Ethan, slowly. Greyson cuts in quickly before he can say anything else.

"So I won't be back for Thanksgiving unless Ben can pull off some sort of miracle."

"Yeah, I heard," says Ethan. "So listen, Emily and I were talking. I think we're going to drive up with the kids and spend the holiday with you. Mom and Dad are out of town anyway, Emily's folks have her brother over so they won't miss us, and I wouldn't mind getting eyes on the house before we sell it."

A wide smile breaks out across Greyson's face. He looks delighted at the prospect of getting to spend the holiday with Ethan and his family after all. I guess the feeling is infectious because I find myself smiling despite how mopey I've been all morning.

"Great!" says Greyson. "That's… thanks, Ethan. That's really cool of you."

"Pfft, I just wanna see the house. I only said that other bit to make you feel better."

Greyson laughs.

"You're a dick."

"No," says Ethan. "I'll tell you who's a dick. Peterson is a dick. Have you called him yet?"

I feel like I'm being let in on some big family secret. But Greyson stiffens, visibly irritated at the mention of Peterson's name.

"I've been sick," says Greyson, defensively.

"You've called people before when you're sick. I know he's a lot of work but… call him. You know how he gets."

"I thought you didn't get sick," I whisper. Apparently not quietly enough.

"Is that what he said?" asks Ethan. "He always says that. Just before he gets sick."

I give Greyson a wide, smug grin, and he puts his entire hand over my face and pushes me so I fall backward on the couch, laughing.

"I'll call him," says Greyson.

"All right. He's been making inquiries at ABM, so it's pretty urgent."

"First thing tomorrow," says Greyson.

"Good. See you in a few days. Bye Allie!"

The phone clicks off just as I manage to right myself on the couch and grab my sandwich.

"He seems nice," I say.

"He's the nice brother," says Greyson.

"Low bar," I shoot back, winking, and Greyson rolls his eyes with a smile.

"You know," I go on, as an idea starts to form in my mind. "The kitchen is fine for sandwiches and one-pots, but I'm not sure you'll be able to cook a full Thanksgiving dinner in there."

Greyson looks thoughtful for a moment, and as my observation sinks in his brow draws down into a frown. It's a lovely kitchen, but it's old—the oven is too small and too flaky to entrust with a whole turkey, there's no garbage disposal, and there's some kind of blockage in the pipes that causes the water pressure to suddenly drop without warning. Unless Greyson is planning to cook the entire dinner in the twenty-year-old microwave oven, he's out of luck.

"Hmm," he says, and I can almost hear the cogs ticking over in his head.

"Bring them to Sadie's," I say.

He pauses mid-chew and looks at me.

"Well, you were going to come anyway. It's only, what? Two more adults and two kids? The more the merrier. Sadie won't mind."

He gets an expression on his face like he's having a thousand different thoughts at once, and then he looks at me and just stares for a moment.

"Okay," he says. And then he repeats it like he's surprised to be agreeing. "Okay. If it's all right with Sadie and we're not too much of an imposition."

"Great!" I say. "I'll call her after lunch." I happily tuck into my sandwich again, while Greyson hits play on a comedy show.

❄

By mid-afternoon, having called Sadie and secured her enthusiastic agreement to host yet more people, I'm sitting in one of the huge armchairs reading my Kindle. No matter how hard I try to get into the story of a hapless young woman abducted by an alien warlord who wants to make alien hybrid babies with her—a brand of escapism that's usually right up my alley—I'm back to feeling antsy. I look up every few minutes to check if it's still snowing, and it always is. Greyson is sitting on the couch reading a book of his own. It looks like a thriller. I suspect it features fewer self-lubricating alien penises than mine.

"Right," says Greyson suddenly. He slaps his own book closed, puts it on the table, and gets to his feet.

I look up, watching him with wide eyes as he leaves the room. A short while later he's back, and he throws my coat at me.

"Come on," he says. "I'm sick of watching you sit there being miserable and trying to look like you're not."

He shrugs on his own coat.

"Your kids are fine," he says. "They're better than fine. They're having a blast in the snow with their cousins. And we're going to do the same. Why should they have all the fun?"

I reflexively open my mouth to protest... before realizing that I don't really have a good excuse. Why *should* I be sitting around sighing and worrying, when I know that everything is perfectly fine?. But of course, I don't want him to be right, so instead, I just purse my lips defiantly. He grins back at me, in a way that is simultaneously maddening and hot.

"See?" he says, wrapping his scarf around his neck. "I'm right. Get your coat on."

※

THWAP!

The snowball I launch hits Greyson straight in the side of his face. What started as a short walk around the property, kicking through the snow, quickly escalated into a snowball battle to the death when I couldn't resist grabbing the fluffy white cap from a fence post and throwing it at him.

"You little..." He packs up a snowball of his own and launches it. I duck out of the way just in time, feeling it breeze past my ear before it lands with a quiet thud in the deeper snow behind me.

"HAH!" I shout, victoriously.

I bend over for more snow, grabbing a handful of ammunition with my gloves and packing it together as I move, taking high, long strides to reach cover behind one of the nearby garden sheds.

"Oh, Alliiiiie!" I hear him coming closer and duck down, poised, waiting. As soon as he rounds the corner I let the snowball fly and catch him again.

"Motherf—!" he shouts, wiping the side of his face.

"Surrender!" I call, jumping to my feet.

"Never!" he replies, grabbing up another pile of snow between his hands.

I turn around to run but the snow is so deep and untouched that I struggle through every step.

I'm done for.

The snowball smacks me right in the back of my head and I go down, falling face-first into the snow.

"HAH!" I hear him shout.

A devious grin curls on my lips.

"He shoots, he scores! Face me like a man!" he calls.

It takes everything I have not to laugh. I stay stock still in the snow, not moving a muscle.

"Allie?" He calls. I hear the first slight change in his tone and I know he's bitten. All I have to do now is reel him in.

"Allie?" He's a little closer.

"Allie!" Louder this time, and right beside me. I feel his hand on my arm, and I whip around and smoosh a handful of cold snow into his face.

"Treachery!" he yells. "Cheat!"

I let out a peal of laughter as lay on my back in the snow, and he reaches down and starts tickling me in revenge, just like he did when the ground was unfrozen and we were laying in a puddle of mud by the broken tap.

"Mercy! I give in!" I cry, laughing uncontrollably.

He looks at me again, that same way, his smile fading.

He glances to my lips, and back to my eyes, and just like last time I feel a whirlpool start to churn inside me. I can't tell if I'm more excited or scared.

"Allie," he says.

This is not the same as last time.

"Yes?" I say, but my voice doesn't quite manage to gain purchase on my breath and it comes out as a whisper.

"I'm going to kiss you again," he says, pushing a curl out of my face.

My heart flips over in my chest.

"Okay," I say, giving a little nod.

"Allie," he says again. I move my gaze from his lips to his eyes.

"Yeah?"

"I'm not going to stop."

My heart is hammering—no, flipping—no, somersaulting in my chest. There's no way in hell I'm going to be able to utter anything more than a squeak, so I nod instead.

I nod yes because I want him to kiss me, and I don't want him to stop, and then I feel the warmth of his lips on mine and I let out a quiet moan.

He somehow manages to pull me up a little from the snow and place his hand on the back of my neck, his fingers laced into my hair, and he probes his tongue against my lips until I part them and lean deeper into him.

Nothing has ever felt so natural as the way our tongues dance together, responding to each other with lazy, slow passion.

When he pulls back this time, he does not immediately get to his feet and run away from me. He looks me right in the eye and smiles.

"I want you, Allie," he says, and I bite my bottom lip.

"I wanted you from the moment I saw you in your stupid antlers, pretending to be French."

"Busted!" I say, because all the nervous energy inside me has to come out somehow and I guess this is the escape hatch it chose.

Greyson takes it in his stride, laughing and pressing a gentle kiss to my lips.

"I want to take you to my bed, Allie," he says, His eyes look almost glazed with lust, and as he says it I feel my hips tilting upwards off the snow towards him, betraying my own desire.

"Yes," I say, nodding. "Do. That, I mean. You should do that."

For the love of God, why am I not more sexy? I imagine other women in this situation. They'd be making come-hither looks with their sultry eyes, responding to his propositions with classy-yet-highly-suggestive innuendos in their husky, lust-ragged voices. So far I've managed "Busted!" and something that I don't even think qualifies as a complete sentence.

Greyson doesn't seem to mind. He's smiling at me as he pulls me to my feet. Then, romantically but very unexpectedly, he reaches down to grab the backs of my thighs with one arm and the top of my back with the other, and sweeps me up into his arms.

I let out a little scream and grab around his neck, clinging on for dear life. Have I mentioned that he's very tall?

"I cam fee," he says, and I realize his speech is muffled because I have a death grip on his head and I'm squeezing it into my coat-covered chest.

"What?" I ask, pulling back a bit.

I feel more secure than I'd expected. He's strong, and his thick arms are wrapped underneath me, as solid as the ground itself.

"I couldn't see," he says, looking down at me. His gaze roams all over my face like he's taking in every detail. "You have about ten steps to change your mind, Alora Brooks."

"Quick," I say. "Run!"

He throws his head back and bellows a loud laugh as he carries me inside.

CHAPTER 12

Greyson

Until this very second, "adorably dorky" wasn't even in the top 100 on the list of things I found sexy, and yet here we are and it's shot right to the top. Allie's a little nervous. I can tell by the way she keeps meeting my eyes and then looking away, but I'm transfixed—watching every feature of her face as the emotions wash across them. It's only making me even more eager to get inside her ridiculously oversized coat.

I kick the bedroom door open and set her down on her feet. She stands there with her arms at her sides, chewing on her bottom lip (probably number two on the list now).

I press the side of my index finger against the underside of her chin, forcing her big, green eyes to meet mine, and I lean down and kiss her again. Her scent is honey and flowers and freshly fallen snow, and she tastes divine.

"You're beautiful," I tell her, pulling back. I start to undo her coat, and she takes a breath in. I can tell she's about to pipe up with some self-deprecating comeback, so I press my finger against her lips to silence her.

"Shh," I say. "I said what I said."

She smiles against my finger and I lean in again, kissing around her full lips as I undo the buttons of her coat and peel it off her shoulders. I pull her sweater over her head and discard it, and then I have to pause a moment, just to look at her.

Her jeans are snug around her waist, and her nipples are pebbled underneath the thin, silky fabric of a white bra.

"Oh, Lord," I breathe, moving my hand to her left breast. I cup it, gently, and run my thumb over the peak of her nipple. The whimper from her mouth is like music to my ears.

She reaches up and places her hand on the side of my neck, pulling me toward her, and I gladly follow her lead, flicking my tongue across her lips. My length is straining against my pants, taught and hard, but I'm desperate to see her fall apart before I have my way with her.

I push my fingers into the top of her jeans and yank her toward me, pulling her close so she can feel my hardness pressing into her belly.

"Look what you've done to me," I say, biting her bottom lip gently. She moans into my mouth, all her nervous quips spent.

I move my thumb and fingers on her jeans and flick open her top button, then pull down the zipper and push them down over her hips. She wriggles out of them, kicking her shoes off at the same time. As soon as her legs are free, I lift her up and throw her backward onto the bed, where she lands on her back with a squeal.

I crawl onto the bed after her and she parts her thighs for me until I'm propped up with an arm on either side of her shoulders, looming over her.

"Hello," I say, lowering myself down to kiss her.

Fully clothed, I grind myself against her, my hardness rolling up and down over her sex as her mouth makes a delightful little 'O' shape and her breathing gets just a little harder. Her hands move down, her fingers wriggle against my torso until she gets purchase on my shirt, and she pulls it upward, over my head, and throws it across the room.

"Allie," I say, and her name feels so hot on my lips it's like a curse. "Tell me what you want."

She flushes immediately and pulls me down toward her. She kisses me, her tongue in my mouth, on my lips. She nibbles at my neck and my jaw, and then she whispers into my ear.

"I want you inside me."

Her answer makes my balls lift and my length twitch against her slit, but I have no intention of giving into that particular demand just yet. I unhook her bra and peel it off, and I take a moment to look down at her perfect breasts and her pebbled nipples. I lean down and flick my tongue against one, wetting it, before I pull back and blow gently on it. Her reaction—a lift of her hips that rolls her vulva against my achingly erect dick—tells me everything.

Shifting down the bed a little, I keep my attention on her nipples. I lick and suckle and flick with my tongue until she's squirming and breathless, and then I kiss a trail down her belly and press my thumb against her most sensitive spot, on the outside of her panties.

They match her bra, white and silky, and there is a small dark patch of wet where I've been rubbing against her.

"Holy…" she says, trailing off into a little gasp when I pull her panties to the side and flick my tongue against her clitoris. I use my fingers to open her, gently, and lave my tongue along her slit, bottom to top, before I settle on that sensitive little bud and roll circles around it until she starts to pant.

I slide a finger inside her and hook it, and then another, curling them slightly until her hands slam into the bed on either side of her and she grips at the sheets until her knuckles go white. I can feel her legs start to shake, and I can taste her arousal as it builds and builds.

"Oh my God!" she shouts, louder than I was expecting. I am utterly desperate to be inside her, but there's no chance in hell I'm allowing myself that pleasure until she's had her first orgasm.

Just when I think I can't take any more, she falls apart. Her hips buck, her sex clenches around my fingers, and she moans in time with waves that seem to crash through her entire body. She is beautiful, and I'm enthralled.

I pull my own jeans and underwear off while she lays on the bed, panting, and then I lay down over her, exercising every ounce of self-restraint I have to keep from immediately burying myself inside this beautiful creature underneath me. Her eyes are like satisfied little slits, still rolling slightly with the tail end of her orgasm. As she comes back to her senses, she wraps her legs around my waist and pulls me forward.

For all that I wanted to wait and tease her, my body has other ideas. I let out a loud, guttural groan as I slide effortlessly into her. She is tight and warm and still slightly pulsing, and there's not an ounce of restraint left in me. I loop my arms beneath hers and my hands under her head so I can keep her facing me, and then I begin to rock my hips, staring into her eyes and willing her to feel every ounce of what I feel for her.

She moans as I make love to her. Her eyes roll a little in her head and she grabs around me, her nails digging into my back and her ankles crossing over behind me, as though she wants to keep me deep inside her.

She is everything I expected and more. Her body fits me like a glove and every sound, every move she makes drives me closer and closer to losing myself inside her.

Her lips are beside my ear, whispering, and what she's saying is unintelligible over the sounds of her ragged breaths and mine, but I'm sure it's filthy. Her nails press into my back harder, her legs grip tighter, and I feel her clench, and clench again, and another orgasm rolls through her.

I slam into her, faster and harder, feeling the pressure build inside me, and with a loud groan, I bury myself as deep as I can and spill my seed.

I lay on top of her for a long while, breathless, and I notice almost peripherally that she's running her fingers up and down my back. I twitch, and twitch again, my nerve endings still too sensitive in the aftermath of the orgasm, and after the third twitch, I laugh and grab her hand to stop her.

She's laying there, naked and satisfied with her eyes sparkling in the afterglow, and I roll off her and lay beside her, pulling her into me and wrapping my arms around her.

"Thank you," she whispers, into the quiet, and it's all I can do to stop myself laughing at how ridiculous it is for *her* to be thanking *me*.

"You can thank me after I've made you dinner," I say, and lean down to kiss her temple.

Whatever doubts I've been battling over the past few weeks seem to have vanished, discarded like an old, tattered comfort blanket that's outlived its purpose. As I lay beside Allie, listening to her breathing return to normal and feeling her warm, bare skin against mine, I don't miss it one bit.

❄

I got out of bed to cook this chilli con carne reluctantly, and not before making Allie come again—I'm a gentleman, after all. When I set the plate down in front of Allie and her eyes light up, I feel a little rush of pride.

"Hungry?" I ask.

"Starving," she says, with a devilish little smile.

She tucks in, making a bunch of appreciative noises about the taste of the chilli, and we chat our way through dinner as though we've been together for years. We talk about what sort of furniture the next owners of the house should put in, what color the outside should be painted. She still insists it should be yellow, and I'm still pretty sure I like the classic grey better.

"Well that's just boring," she says, letting her fork drop with a clatter onto her empty plate, and I grin at her.

"It's neutral," I say. "The type of person who wants a yellow house will paint it yellow. The type who wants grey won't even look at a yellow house."

"Nobody likes the grey house people," she says, and I laugh as I clear the plates.

"I can't imagine the people of Sunrise Valley disliking anyone," I say, grabbing a couple of glasses and a bottle of wine.

"That's just because you're not in the gossip network," she informs me. "It's vicious."

I beckon her with a nod of my head and she follows me into the sitting room. I pour us a couple of glasses of wine and we settle in, me leaning against the end of the couch and her between my legs, leaning back against me, as though it's the most natural thing in the world.

"You never thought of living anywhere else?" I ask. Probably a little too hopefully.

She takes a sip of her wine, hesitating over the answer.

"I want the girls to grow up here," she says. "Their cousins are here, their aunt and uncles, extended family..." She shrugs. "They already lost their parents."

"What happened?" I ask. It would have felt like prying before, but I think it's safe to say we've knocked down a few barriers tonight.

"Car crash," she says. "Libby—that's my sister—and her husband Alex... they went off to a wedding. Emma was only a couple of months old. Libby didn't want to leave her, but it was a close friend and I was home from college, so I said I'd watch them."

I can feel the emotion building inside her. The horror. The sadness. I squeeze her tighter against me and stay silent.

"They were late home. I didn't think much of it. Then the cops showed up a little after midnight."

I suck in a breath, close my eyes, already knowing what's coming. Allie talks as though she's on autopilot, swirling the wine around in her glass.

"The driver of the semi that hit them was diabetic, and he'd skipped his medicine. He passed out and the truck jackknifed across the highway, right into Libby and Alex's car."

I place my glass down so I can wrap both arms around her.

"I'm so sorry, Allie."

"It's been three years," she says. "I still get sad about it sometimes, but I have the girls to keep me busy. And I have to do a good job with them or Libby will haunt me. She was the type."

"If she was half as stubborn as you, I can believe it," I say, gently. "And I think you're doing a great job." I hesitate to press on, but since she's opened up about it... "But how come you ended up raising the girls? You must have only been... what? Twenty?"

"Twenty-one," she says. "And it's because Libby had put me in her will as the girls' guardian if anything happened to them. I guess they had to put someone down, and it was probably just a way of giving me a mention. Like an honorary godmother. I doubt it even crossed her mind that it would ever actually happen."

"But it did," I say.

"It did. Sadie and Eddie offered to take them in, but it was my name on the will. So it's my responsibility."

There's that stubbornness again. I can't help but be impressed by how much resolve she packs into her tiny frame.

"It's a lot to take on," I note, running my fingers up and down her arm. She lays her hand over mine and nods.

"It is, but I wouldn't change it."

"You were at college?" I ask. "Doing what?"

"Art school."

"Oh," I say, sitting up a little. "Cartoons?"

She half-turns to look at me with a curious little frown on her face.

"How did you know?"

"I knocked your bag off the chair," I say, nodding towards it. "And a few papers fell out."

She fixes me with the same devilish grin. "Doing recon on your target, were you?"

"I plead the fifth!"

She smiles again. I love the fact that I seem to be able to lighten her mood when she needs it.

"You're really talented. And I say that as someone who sees about a dozen art-school applicants a month," I say. "Have you thought about taking it back up again?"

"Yeah. I have a decent portfolio and I've applied to a few places, but it's not very often that the newspapers around here get any openings, you know?"

"What about starting a webcomic or something?"

She gives a little laugh. "No, no. I figured I wouldn't have the time. I'm lucky that my parents basically gave me their house after we lost Libby. They moved into a retirement village a few towns over. But it's still a struggle to provide for the girls. And I'm not generally in the mood to draw after I've pulled one shift at the diner and another at the bar, y'know?"

I don't know. I haven't got the foggiest clue how she does what she does, and without so much as a complaint. She's a hero. And now, she's my hero.

We chat a little longer, and then we head up to bed. I make love to her more slowly this time, taking pains to explore every inch of her body with my lips and my tongue and my fingers, and when we eventually collapse, exhausted, I wrap my arms around her body and pull her close. For the first time in as long as I can remember, I am content.

"Oh, look, Greyson," she says, as she drifts off to sleep in my arms. I follow her gaze to the window.

"It's not snowing anymore."

CHAPTER 13

Allie

I feel like my feet are barely touching the ground, and I'm pretty sure that everyone else can see it as well. I've been floating around the diner all day with a particularly sunny smile on my face, but the shift was so busy that Sam hasn't had a chance to interrogate me yet. He's just been giving me an occasional, suspicious side-eye as we pass each other en route to the next table. Until now.

"You've had sex!" he says, narrowing his eyes at me as he leans his butt against the counter and watches me clearing off some plates.

I glance up at him, then back down as I scrape off the final plate into the bin.

"You're supposed to be washing dishes," I say.

"Bet!" he calls, as our boss breezes into the kitchen with plates stacked a foot high on each arm. How the hell she never drops any is beyond me.

"Yes, dear?" she says, placing the plates down and scraping them off.

"Allie's had sex!"

"Oh, that's nice," she says, pushing the pile of plates toward Sam. He takes the hint, turns around, and starts rinsing them off and stacking the dishwasher. Bet gives me a wink and heads back out the door, leaving me to finish scraping off the plates she collected.

"So," says Sam, clearly not willing to let this go. "Fact 1: you've definitely had sex. Fact 2: the only eligible man that's come into your life recently is Jawline McPecs. And Fact 3: you just spent three days trapped with him in that big old mansion. In conclusion," he whirls around, jabbing the dish brush at me as if it were Sherlock Holmes' pipe, "J'accuse! You've been having a scandalous love affair with your boss!"

I can't hold it off anymore. A smirk crawls onto my lips, and Sam practically explodes.

"OH MY GOD, YOU DID! You filthy animal, I'm so proud of you. Is he amazing in bed? Or in the shower? Or on the kitchen countertop? Exactly how many places did you two do it anyway, you insatiable wench?"

"Wash the dishes!" I say, still grinning, as I push through the kitchen doors and head back into the dining room to help Bet. The place is pretty empty now, except for a few stragglers, and it's almost time to shut up shop. After that, we'll be spending the next few hours peeling the vegetables for tomorrow's Thanksgiving dinner.

Greyson will be here any minute to help, and every time I think about the fact that I'm going to see him again, my tummy feels like I've gone over a hill too fast. I haven't seen him since I left the mansion the morning after we got down and dirty. He's been busy getting the house ready and I've been busy working in the diner and catching up on the time I missed with the girls.

He sent me a message yesterday on the HelpForHire site, demanding my number and telling me it was ridiculous that he had to contact "his woman" this way. He was being facetious, but it still made me tingle in places that, until recently, haven't tingled in a long time. And then he sent me a text to say he'd only be able to stay a few hours because his brother arrives tonight.

"So is he all muscles and tan?" asks Sam, pursuing me out of the kitchen, clearly having decided that the dishes can damn well wait.

I roll my eyes and shove a couple of empty mugs at him.

"You're so nosy!"

"So are you!" he contests. "Remember when I first started dating Drew? You didn't stop asking me questions for three weeks. *Three weeks*, Allie. And now you're *starving* me!"

He's so dramatic. But he's not wrong. I am starving him. Because this thing with Greyson, whatever it is, feels special. It feels right that only he and I know about it, and I don't feel the need to gossip about it the way I have with other flings, back in the years before I inherited a couple of preschoolers.

"He'll be here soon," I say. "Ask him yourself."

Sam's jaw drops theatrically, and I snort a laugh as I push his chin back up.

"Here? Like, *here* here? In the diner?"

"Yeah," I shrug. "He's coming to help us prep for tomorrow."

"No shit," says Sam, his brows raising in surprise.

"Yes shit," I reply. "And he's coming to Sadie's for dinner tomorrow."

Sam's brows hitch up a little further.

"With his brother and sister-in-law and their kids."

It's too much. Sam's eyebrows all but disappear into his hairline and his mouth makes no less than six different shapes before he manages to speak again.

"I *can't even* with you," he says, with (mostly) feigned disgust. "You've been holding out on me all day, when you could, at any time, have shared this treasure trove of gossip with me?" He shakes his head slowly, thoroughly disappointed in me. "You've changed, Allie."

"I don't think it counts as gossip if I'm the subject, Sam," I grin back.

"It's gossip if you're having sex with some tall dark Adonis all over a mansion!" he says.

And then the sound of a clearing throat makes us both freeze. We spin around at the same time and sure enough, there's Greyson, standing a little ways behind us, looking just absolutely divine in his long coat.

"Hey!" I say.

I don't know the rules, and I suddenly find myself panicking a bit. Am I supposed to hug him? Kiss him? Elbow bump? *What are the rules?*

I don't even need to look at Sam to know that he's watching this scene unfold like a hawk.

Greyson breezes across the room, an amused look on his face, places his hand on my hip, and leans down to peck a soft kiss to my cheek.

"Hey yourself," he smiles back warmly.

Oh. I guess those are the rules. I can definitely work with that.

Greyson goes to hang up his coat, and as soon as he's not looking in our direction anymore, Sam clasps his hands together and makes an over-the-top "awwwwwwwwwww" face, like Greyson and I are just the sweetest thing he's ever seen. I'd love to play it cool, but I can't. I grin right back at him like a total dork, and we both have to quickly straighten our faces as Greyson turns back to face us.

"So," says Greyson, rolling up his sleeves (hot). "Where shall I start? Dishes?"

"Apron," I say, reaching into a drawer to pull one out. "Sam can handle the rest of the dishes, and Bet will be here in a minute to tell us all what to do."

"Don't worry," says Sam. "She's good at that." He wipes his hand on his apron and holds it out toward Greyson. "Sam, by the way. Allie's closest confidant, most hardworking colleague, and favorite in-law."

"Oh, that's right," says Greyson, shaking his hand. "Sadie's brother?"

Sam gives me a recriminating glare. "Has *everyone* in town met him before me?"

Greyson shakes his head. "Not at all. You were here the first day I arrived, with the French girl. Did she quit?"

Sam stares blankly at Greyson for a moment, then he glances at me and it clicks. He laughs, shaking his head.

"No, she still works here. But she keeps secrets and gossip to herself so we're not friends anymore."

Greyson lets out a laugh, and I roll my eyes at both of them. But I can't keep a smile from creeping onto my face as well.

"Oh, you must be Gary!" calls Bet, poking her head out from the kitchen.

"Greyson!" the three of us say in unison.

"All right, all right, keep your hair on!" says Bet, chuckling. "And come on through to the back, there's a lot to get done."

❄

Sam was right—Bet definitely is good at telling us what to do. Carrots here, parsnips there, don't put crosses in the wrong end of the brussels sprouts. It's practically a military operation.

Sam puts on some festive music in the background and we all chat our way through the next couple of hours, until there are pots full of veg and pans full of sauce on every ring of every stove, and every oven has a turkey ready to start cooking tomorrow morning.

"Well, we've done it again," says Bet, bringing in a bottle of sherry from the pantry. I'm pretty sure it's the same bottle that she had when I first started working at the diner. She only ever brings it out the night before Thanksgiving, when everything is done. She pours us all a good measure while we peel off our aprons and put away the last of the cutlery.

"Here's to us," she says, lifting her glass. "And since I won't see you tomorrow, I'm thankful for all your help. And for you two," she says, looking at me first, then Sam. "For all the hard work you do here. I don't know how I'd manage without you. "And you," she says, turning to Greyson. "For whatever you did to Allie to make her as happy as she's been the last few days."

I feel my cheeks get hot as she says it. I've definitely noticed that I feel a little lighter and a little less haggard than before, but I didn't realize it was *that* obvious.

"I bet it was filthy," says Sam, eyeing Greyson up and down.

I see a wide grin appear on Greyson's face as he looks right at Sam.

"The mansion?" asks Greyson, casually. "Yeah, it was pretty dirty when I first arrived."

"What are you thankful for, Allie?" asks Bet, obviously trying to stop Sam from clarifying his meaning. I glance immediately at Greyson, then look away and give the same answer I've given for the last three years.

"I'm thankful for the girls, and for my family."

It's true. There were more than a few times, that first year, when I was woken up in the middle of the night by the horrifying thought that the girls could have been in the car as well. Losing my sister was bad enough. Losing the girls, too, would have broken me. There's a part of me that believes everything happens for a reason. Maybe Libby and Alex granting me custody is the only reason I'm still functioning after the loss of a sister who was also my best friend.

I'm suddenly aware that the air has become heavy. I'm so busy, day to day, that the time before the accident often feels like another lifetime, but it's only been three years. It's still so fresh, really, that whenever I mention my family it's the first thing that pops into people's heads.

Greyson reaches over and grabs my hand, giving it a tight squeeze.

"Well *I'm* thankful for Sherry," Sam pipes up, lifting up his glass, and we all break out in grateful laughter that chases away the tension.

"And I'm thankful I'll be seeing my brother tonight," says Greyson, checking his watch. He looks down at me. "I'd better head off, they'll be arriving soon if the traffic was good. Walk you to your car?"

"Sure." I nod, and I head over to give Bet a tight squeeze. "I hope everything goes all right tomorrow. Call me if you need anything."

"You go on," says Bet, returning my hug and then shooing me away. "Enjoy your time with the girls. God knows you deserve it. And you, young man," she looks up to Greyson. "You look after this one. She's a good girl."

"Yes, ma'am," says Greyson with a nod. And even though it's the only response he could have given, he looks very serious when he says it.

❄

As soon as we're outside, Greyson grabs my wrist and pulls me around, pushing me gently but firmly against the back wall of the diner. His lips meet mine instantly, and his warm hand cups the side of my face. He feels every bit as good as I remember. I kiss him back, grabbing the front of his coat with both hands and pulling him closer. It's really some sort of cruel and unusual punishment that circumstances have kept us apart ever since our night (and morning) of passion.

"God, I wish I could bring you home tonight," he says, his forehead pressed against mine when he finally breaks the kiss.

"Me, too," I say, nodding.

"You know it's going to kill me tomorrow, being with you all day and not being able to touch you?" he asks.

I do know. I've thought about him so many times over the last few days that I'm not sure where my memories of his sculpted body end and my fantasies about it begin.

"At least we'll be together," I say. "And it'll be nice to meet your brother. I'm sure he's got plenty of dirt on you."

"Hey!" Greyson scolds, bopping me gently on the tip of my nose with the knuckle of his index finger. "No snooping!"

I laugh, and he pulls me away from the wall and takes my hand to walk me to the car. The way his fingers slide between mine, skin against skin, slotting perfectly, easily into place, is almost as intimate as the memory of him slotting between my thighs.

"See you tomorrow, then?" he says when we get to my car. He lifts my hand up and kisses it, then leans down to brush his lips lightly across mine again.

"Dinner at two," I remind him. "Well, Sadie says that to get everyone there on time, but we normally eat closer to three. But don't tell her I told you."

Greyson grins and does a little two-finger salute. "Scout's honor," he says, and leans down to open the door for me to get into my car.

CHAPTER 14

Greyson

"Look who it is!" I grin as my brother and his wife, Emily, pull into the driveway and get out of their car. I keep my voice low—the kids are both in the back seat, fast asleep. "Welcome to the sticks." I pull them both into a bear hug. I really have missed them.

"Wow," says Ethan, looking up at the mansion with an appreciative nod. "The place is looking pretty good."

"Yeah, it's starting to come together," I nod. "Can I get you two a drink? Tea? Water? Wine?"

Emily shakes her head. "Not for me. I'm going to get these two to bed and then turn in myself. Can you show us to our room, Greyson?"

"Sure," I say, beckoning them into the house.

They each take one of the children from the backseat, carrying them gingerly into the house and up the stairs to their room. The kids barely stir—they must really be exhausted from the trip. Once the kids are tucked in and Emily has bid us goodnight, Ethan and I sit in the kitchen with two glasses of scotch.

"So how much work do you have left, you think?" he asks, looking around.

"Dunno," I say, noncommittal, shrugging my shoulder. "A few weeks."

Ethan eyes me across the table, one brow lifted, and then quietly sips his scotch.

"So you like her, huh?" he says.

Aaaaand now I remember what the downsides of having your older brother around are. They see right through your bullshit, even if you've managed to fool yourself. There's no point in denying it or playing dumb, so instead my face just breaks into a wide grin.

"Oh man, you've got it bad, huh?" Ethan grins right back at me.

"She's nice," I say with a shrug.

"She'd have to be," Ethan says. "I haven't seen you this smitten since Olivia."

As soon as he says that name, my smile drops.

Olivia was my first proper girlfriend. We were inseparable all through high school. She was beautiful and kind and funny and smart, and I ruined her. I know that sounds dramatic, but it's the truth.

I didn't have to go to college. Ethan had already started the company with some of our inheritance. I could have gone straight in after high school and started working my way up, stayed at home, stayed with Olivia. But I had this idea in my head that going off to college on your own was a rite of passage and a great adventure, and I wasn't prepared to give that up. Not even for her. She begged me to stay. But I didn't.

By the time I got back, Olivia was a shell of her former self. She'd fallen in with the wrong crowd, and all that was left of her was skin and bone, sunken eyes, and track marks. There was nothing I could do to save her. God knows I tried. For two long, soul-destroying years I tried. And then, after the umpteenth relapse and the umpteen-and-first tearful promise that next time would be different, I had to walk away for the sake of my sanity. Last I heard of her, she was living in some homeless shelter downtown and turning tricks for hits.

"G?"

I look up at him, snapping out of my reverie and forcing a smile.

Olivia was a long time ago. And maybe I'm starting to convince myself that it doesn't have to be that way again. Maybe I do deserve to be happy. Maybe I'm not just destined to hurt people. I sure as shit don't believe for a second that I'd ever hurt Allie or the girls.

"Yeah," I say, nodding. "Yeah, she's pretty special. It's nothing official, though. We're just getting to know each other, you know?"

Ethan nods. Much to my relief, he doesn't press it any further.

"So I guess you won't be back in the city until Christmas?"

"Probably not," I say.

"Did you call Peterson yet?"

A wave of irritation rises in my gut at the mention of his name. At myself, that is. It's not like me to put things off the way I'm putting off talking to Peterson, but every time Allie pops into my head, ten other things seem to fall out.

"No. I'll do it."

Ethan frowns at me a little. "He's starting to get real impatient and he's our biggest client, Greyson. I know he's an asshole, but—"

"I'll do it," I insist again. Ethan pauses for a moment, giving me an uncertain look, and then changes the subject to football.

❄

"Morning!"

Emily breezes into the kitchen the next morning and pecks a kiss on my cheek.

"Hey," I grin. "Have a seat."

"Something smells good," she says, taking a deep sniff through her nose as she perches on the other side of the breakfast bar.

This kitchen may not be great for cooking a full Thanksgiving meal, but nobody can cook as much breakfast food in a single pan as me. They might as well crown me King of the Bachelors.

"It'll taste even better, I *gar-on-tee*!" I say the last bit in an over-the-top French accent, and immediately smile as Allie pops back into my head. "Ethan and the kids coming down?"

"Yeah," she says. "He's helping them through an existential crisis about which socks to wear. They'll be down in a sec."

I laugh at the thought of Ethan wrangling the two kids upstairs. It's so great to have them all here.

"So..." Emily continues, "We're going to Allie's for dinner, huh?"

"Is that your new girlfriend?" calls Leo, my nephew, entering the room. He's seven, and the grin on his face tells me he finds this whole girlfriend thing hilarious.

"Morning, squirt," I say.

"Greyson's got a girlfriend! Greyson's got a girlfriend!" he sings, skipping around in a circle.

His sister, Riley, is three. She doesn't understand why Leo is so excited, but as soon as she sees him skipping around in a circle, she joins in.

"Come on," says Ethan, entering the kitchen behind them. He looks just the way you'd expect a man who's just refereed a sock battle to look. "Sit down at the table."

He moves behind Emily and leans down to kiss the top of her head.

"Morning, sweetheart." He looks up to me and nods. "Morning."

"What, no 'sweetheart'?" I grin back.

"Greyson's got a girlfriend!" sings Ethan.

"Leo, Riley, sit at the table, please," says Emily. "And stop singing."

I turn to the stove and start moving things around with my spatula. There's hash browns, sausages, tomatoes, and in a separate pan, I'm scrambling some eggs.

"So you do have a girlfriend?" asks Emily.

I turn around to stare at her, deadpan.

"Et tu, Emily? I thought you were on my side!"

"I'm on the side of the truth," she grins, and I shake my head.

"Well it's none of your business," I say. "Any of you." I point my spatula at Leo. "Especially you."

He pokes his tongue out at me and blows a raspberry.

I start loading the food onto plates and flick the coffee machine on.

"We're going to dinner at Sadie's house," I say. "That's Allie's sister-in-law. She invited me over when my flight was canceled, and then Allie asked if she could take a few more when I found out you guys were coming up."

"That's really nice of them," says Emily.

"They're nice people," I say, and I mean it. It's different here than in the city. And I mean, completely different. I get smiles from some of these people just passing them on the street that are wider and brighter than I'd get from neighbors I've seen every day for five years back home.

"So who else is gonna be there?" asks Ethan.

"Let's see. Sadie and her husband, Eddie. They have a couple of kids I think but I don't remember their names. And then there's Sam—he works at the diner with Allie and he's Sadie's brother—"

"Everyone knows everyone, huh?" says Emily. She's from a small town herself, originally, and the look in her eyes is half wistful.

"Something like that," I say. "And then there's Sam's boyfriend, I think he's called Andrew? And Allie and the girls."

"The girls?" asks Ethan, and I catch him and Emily exchanging a quick glance when I turn around.

"Yes," I say, picking up the plates and heading over to the table with them. "She has two girls. Lottie and Emma. She adopted them."

"Oh," says Ethan.

Emily is just blinking at me, not sure how to respond.

"They were her sister's," I say.

I don't want to say she died in front of the kids and set off another, far more significant existential crisis, so I opt for more cryptic language: "Accident."

Ethan's face falls, and Emily instinctively leans over to squeeze Riley, who's sitting beside her.

"What about her parents? Allie's, I mean. Will they be there?" she asks.

I shake my head. "They're in a retirement village a few towns over that got snowed in the same time we did, but it hasn't cleared yet. They're gonna go to the village's Thanksgiving dinner instead and come here for Christmas."

"Oh, that's a shame," says Emily. She looks down, clearly still rattled by the thought of the tragedy that befell Allie's family, and a somber silence settles on the room.

"Well, dig in everyone!" I say, in an effort to lighten the mood, and I head back to get the coffee.

By the time breakfast is done and the dishes are washed by hand—I really do need to find a plumber—it's after noon. We spend an hour in the sitting room, chatting and playing some of the games the kids have brought along from home. Leo triumphs at the pizza card game where you have to collect all the different toppings, and Riley is surprisingly good at Jenga, for a tiny kid with chubby fingers.

"So Allie is…" says Emily, once the games are tidied away and Riley has fallen asleep in her lap.

"More than just the woman who's helping him clean up this place, judging by the spring in his step," says Ethan.

"She's nice," I say with a shrug.

"She's his *giiiiiiiirlfriend*," calls Leo, from where he's sitting on the other side of the room, playing with his dad's phone.

"Button it, Leo," says Ethan. "And you'd better be good this afternoon. Don't embarrass your uncle in front of his new girlfriend."

All three of them burst into gales of laughter, and all I can do is smile and shake my head, defeated.

It really is great to have them here.

❄

"Welcome, welcome, welcome!" says Sadie as she opens the door. She's smiling widely, if a little manically, wearing an apron that says THE BOSS across the front, and she has a dishtowel draped over her shoulder.

"Come in, come in. We're still waiting on Sam and Drew, but if you go through, Eddie will get you some drinks. Just in there." She points at a door leading left off the hallway. "I'll be there in a minute. My rutabaga's going to burn!"

She rushes off to the kitchen, and I notice that Emily is grinning. This is just her sort of atmosphere.

I lead everyone through to the living room, and the first thing I see is Allie, standing on the far side of the room, setting out nibbles and glasses and chatting to Eddie. The early afternoon light is coming in from outside and making the crests of her curls glow. She's wearing a pale green blouse that brings out the color of her eyes and she's paired it with skinny jeans and boots, and when she turns and notices me, a wide smile breaks out across her face. As she makes her way across the room towards me, I realize she's wearing just a little more makeup than normal.

She is stunning.

"Hey!" she says, leaning up to kiss me on the cheek. I guess I did set the rules the other night.

"Hey," I say. "This is Ethan, Emily, Leo, and Riley. Everyone, this is—"

"Allie!" Ethan cuts in, grabbing her hand and shaking it enthusiastically. "We've heard *so* much about you!"

Goddamn Ethan, he just can't resist a chance to troll me. Allie's eyes go a little wider, and she starts to blush and she reaches for a response.

"OH! Well, I... er—I hope the drive wasn't too bad!"

I sent her a text last night, lamenting the fact that we'd have been able to get some time together if I knew that Ethan and Emily would be arriving so late. She reminded me quite firmly that she was busy helping Sadie, and then added a load of kissy emojis that made me too happy to be irritated any more. God, what kind of sap have I become?

"It sucked!" says Ethan.

Emily digs him in the ribs.

"It was just fine," she says, shaking Allie's hand. "Thanks, Allie."

The kids only manage a quick hello before they're off, having spotted Allie's girls and Sadie's kids playing some kind of board game in the corner of the room. They immediately insert themselves into the fray, chatting and playing together in that effortless way that kids do.

"Drink?" says Eddie, coming over to our little group. "Drink? Drink? Drink?" He points to each of us in turn and makes a little drinking motion as though he's holding a glass. "There's a pretty decent selection over there on the table."

We head over that way and everyone grabs a drink. Beers all around except for Emily, who opts for water because she's driving us all home later. Allie goes off to distribute juice boxes to the kids, and Eddie gives my hand a bone-crushing shake.

"Nice to finally meet you," he says, with a nod. "How's the old house?"

"Great," I say. "It's really coming along."

"It's a beautiful building," says Emily. "Don't you think?"

"Oh, yeah," says Eddie. "Something of a landmark around here. You pass that house when you're a kid, you know you're almost home. You're selling it on?" Eddie asks, looking back at me.

I'm acutely aware of Ethan and Emily's eyes on me, and of the fact that my head isn't doing what I want it to. I meant to nod, but instead, I'm doing some half-nod, half-shake sort of a thing. Probably because the idea of finishing the house, selling it, and heading back to the city is becoming less appealing by the day.

BING BONG!

I'm saved, literally, by the bell.

"That'll be Sam and Drew. 'Scuse me," says Eddie, squeezing between Emily, Ethan, and myself en route to the door.

I introduce Sam to everyone and he, of course, charms them at once—though he seems a little more subdued than usual. But we barely have a chance to get acquainted before Sadie calls us through to the dining room. All eight adults are seated around the main table, with the kids' table just beside it.

The spread is amazing, with the turkey taking pride of place in the middle of the table. Everyone ooos and aaaaahs at Sadie, and I can't tell if she's flushed from the heat of the kitchen or blushing from the praise. Eddie stands up to carve and serve while the rest of us chat among ourselves.

I love it.

Look, I wasn't expecting any of this. I was expecting to come to Sunrise Valley, hate everything about the place, send regular emails to Ethan about shitty WiFi, get the house finished, and go home, relieved to be back where I belong.

But my own place is dead compared to this. Clinical. Minimalist and cold and barely more than a place to eat and sleep. Compared to this house, alive with children's laughter and talk and the scent of fresh bread and turkey, my place looks like a fancy motel.

I'm not sure that's what I want anymore. And I'm having a harder and harder time convincing myself that I don't deserve more, lately.

"Sam's quiet, isn't he?" Allie whispers. Sadie was very insistent that everyone sit in their assigned seats, and she made sure to put Allie right beside me.

"Yeah," I say, looking over to Sam, who's quietly eating his meal and has barely said a single sarcastic thing since he arrived.

"What about you? You okay?" she asks. I feel her hand slide under the table and close over mine, and she gives me a gentle squeeze.

"Yeah," I nod, smiling as I turn to look her in the eye. "Never better."

CHAPTER 15

Allie

Sadie is positively glowing after dinner. Everything was delicious, everything went smoothly, everyone had a great time, and she knows it.

"Someone's happy," I grin at her, as I head to the kitchen to help her stack the dishwasher.

"Well, duh. It's a miracle I pulled that off. I was so nervous!" she laughs.

"You should've let me help out today, not just with the prep last night. You've barely had a moment to sit down all day." I say, almost apologetically.

"Yeah, I know. But you've been so busy for the last few weeks, I didn't want to give you *another* job. And besides, I obviously didn't need any help." She winks at me, and I grin.

"True," I say. "You're a master of your craft."

"So… they're all really lovely," she says, purposely not looking at me. She busies herself with moving plates and cups about, but she goes on all the same. "Greyson's brother and his wife. Aren't they?"

"Oh my God," I grin. "You said his name! What happened to Something McWhateverpants?"

She snorts. "Well, he's a guest now. And since you seem completely smitten…"

"I am not!" I protest.

She raises a brow at me, knowingly, and all I can do is blush. Elder sisters, man. They see right through your bullshit. Libby was exactly the same way.

"They're lovely," I say, trying to get this conversation back on a less embarrassing track.

"Oh, nicely avoided," she croons, sounding impressed. "Ten out of ten."

I laugh and grab a handful of bubbles from the sink, flicking them at her, and they land right in the middle of her forehead. She gasps and looks shocked for a moment, then grabs the dish towel that's been draped over her shoulder all day and flicks me with it.

"Out!" she shouts, as I jump away with a hoot and a laugh. "Out of my kitchen!"

I grin at her and she nods toward the door. "Go on, I've got this. Go and spend some time with Greyson and his family. We'll be heading for our walk soon, anyway."

The walk is a tradition. I'm not sure how far back it goes, but every Thanksgiving afternoon, once we've had enough time to let our dinner settle a bit, we all head out for a walk up to the summit of the hill that sits just behind the house.

"All right," I agree. "If you're sure."

"Get!" she says, flicking the towel toward me again.

I'm still grinning as I head back into the sitting room. Every chair and seat is full. Emily is sitting on Ethan's lap, Drew is sitting on the arm of Sam's chair, Greyson and Eddie are on opposite ends of the couch. The children are still happily playing together, and Leo and River, Eddie's eight-year-old, seem to have bonded over being the "big kids."

"Allie!" says Drew, when he sees me come in. "Hey, doll. Did I tell you I adore your blouse?"

Drew is awesome. He's lived in town for about a decade now, another transplant from the city looking for a quieter life. He had some trouble adjusting at first until he started working as an apprentice mechanic in the auto-repair shop, and then he seemed to settle right in. He's worked there ever since. He and Sam got together about four years ago and, while nobody would have thought to put them together before that, it turns out that they're basically a perfect couple.

"Oh," I say, looking down at it. "Thanks, Drew. I got it from Maisy's, I think. That little boutique on Main Street."

"Well you look great," he says. "You're glowing." He flicks his gaze to Greyson and back to me, and I feel another flush rising on my cheeks.

Sam, much to my surprise, doesn't take the opportunity to say something sarcastic or embarrassing. He's been my best friend since we were in sixth grade and I seriously can't remember a time when he's passed up an opportunity to act the clown. But there he is, sitting quietly with his right leg bouncing up and down like he's nervous.

"Sit here," says Greyson, getting to his feet and offering me his seat.

"Oh, no." I shake my head. "Thank you, though. We'll be heading out for a walk in a little while."

"A walk?" asks Leo, looking up from the phone he and River are sharing.

"It's trashon!" calls Lottie from the other side of the room. She's sitting with Riley, Emma, and Finn, playing with a collection of dinosaurs and dolls.

"Tradition," I correct her, and she nods.

"Yeah. Trashon."

"You're welcome to come," I tell Greyson, and glance at Ethan and Emily to include them in the invitation. "We just head up the hill out there and watch the sun go down. My grandma always said that even when you find yourself struggling to be thankful for anything, you can go up there and look out at a beautiful sunset and be thankful for that. So we do it every year."

"That's a great idea," says Ethan. "We'll come."

Emily nods beside him, smiling.

Greyson is still on his feet beside me, and when I look up to him he nods.

"I'm in."

He looks amazing today. He has a fair bit of stubble along his square jaw and he's wearing a chunky knit sweater that makes me want to curl up against him. And there's an extra sparkle in his eye. I'm pretty sure it's because his family is in town, which is adorable.

"Great!" I say. "It'll probably be a while before we go, though. There's no rush."

❋

"Lottie! Emma! Come and get dressed right now, we're in a rush!"

The room has been a flurry of activity ever since Sadie breezed in and announced that we'll be going for our walk in ten minutes, otherwise we'll miss the sunset—and all the parents, myself included, immediately realized that's barely enough time to get the kids into their coats and gloves. Especially when they're all in the same room together.

"Wrong sleeve, Emma, darling," I say when I notice she's trying to put her coat on upside down.

Greyson is standing in the middle of the chaos as it swirls around him, looking bemused and amused and also very, very hot. I'm all for tradition, but I'd much rather be climbing him than the hill out back.

Once everyone's ready, we head out, jump over the gate behind the house, and start to head towards "the mountain." Eddie and Sadie insist on calling it that, like it's a point of pride for them, but really it's just a big hill.

There are still patches of snow here and there, and the kids hone in on them. Greyson is walking along beside me with his fingers laced between mine, but he breaks the hold when Leo tosses a half-soggy snowball at him, and sprints toward the squealing child, who runs off up the hill.

"Hey," says Emily, catching up to walk alongside me.

"Oh, hey," I reply, smiling at her.

"You have a lovely town here," she says. "I'm from one just like it. Out in Pennsylvania, though."

"Oh really?" I say, my brows lifting with surprise. "I didn't know."

"Yup. I still miss it sometimes, especially during the holidays."

"You moved to the city to be with Ethan?" I ask, my chest suddenly a little tighter. I hate asking the question because I hate what it implies. I like Greyson. I really, really like Greyson an awful lot. But I don't want to move the girls out of Sunrise Valley and away from their family.

"No," she says, shaking her head and smiling. "I moved to the city to work in finance. I met Ethan when I already lived there."

"Oh," I say, nodding. "I see."

I don't know if it's better or worse that her situation was so different from mine.

"So you still work in finance?" I ask.

"God, no," she says. "I didn't still work in finance when I met Ethan. It wasn't for me. I started a business selling smellies on Etsy, and it sort of took off.

"Smellies?" I ask.

"You know. Wax melts, diffusers, that sort of thing. And then I went to Ethan's company for help with marketing, and it became pretty clear while we were working together that there was a spark between us. He waited until our business was done, and then he asked me out the very same evening. And here we are."

"Awww, how romantic!" I croon. "And that's really cool, that you started your own business."

She smiles, a little bashfully, but clearly proud of her success. "Yeah. And it basically runs itself now, so I get plenty of time with the kids."

"That's great," I say, and I mean it. If I could do something like that, life would be so much easier. It's not that I don't love working at Bet's. It's that I hate being away from the girls.

"So… you must be pretty special, Allie," she goes on. "I've never seen Greyson so happy."

I look over to where he is, grabbing up handfuls of snow as ammunition. All the kids have started attacking him with slush, and Ethan, Sam, and Drew have joined in. It's grownups against kids, and it's not looking good for the grownups.

"Really?" I ask.

"Mmmhmm. Never even known him to have a girlfriend."

"Well, I don't know if I'd call myself that…" I say.

We haven't had that talk yet. I'm not sure either of us is ready for it. The prospect of Greyson leaving once the house is finished is still looming over us, and we're doing our best to ignore it.

"Well, whatever you are. You're good for him. He's been so hard on himself since…" she trails off.

"Since what?" I ask, pulling my gaze back to Emily and slowing my stride.

"Nothing," she says, shaking her head. "I shouldn't say…"

I frown at her, wondering what awful secret Greyson might be harboring. Emily notices my mind working overtime and sighs.

"I really shouldn't have said anything. Look, it's nothing huge. He had a girlfriend when he was younger. He broke it off to go off to college and she got into some trouble. Drugs."

"Oh, no," I say.

"Yeah. He spent the next few years trying to fix her, and... well, you know how that goes with addicts."

I just nod in response. I don't really know, not first-hand, but there's enough conventional wisdom built up around addiction that I can make my own assumptions.

"And I just don't think he ever forgave himself for it. Until now, maybe."

She falls silent as we notice Greyson break off from the snowball fight and start jogging over towards us.

"What are you two talking about?" he says as he reaches us, breathing heavily.

"Oh, I was just telling her all your secrets," says Emily, lightly, and she gives me a wink. "Had enough, Greyson?"

"Oh, yeah," he says, bent over with his hands on his knees, panting. "I'm no glutton for punishment. They beat us, hands down."

"I'd better go make sure the kids aren't getting into too much trouble," says Emily, giving my arm a little squeeze. "Great talking to you, Allie."

As she heads off, Greyson straightens up and grabs my hand, lacing his fingers between mine again. A warm glow swells up inside me and I lean into him, landing a kiss on his upper arm. I don't mention anything that Emily said, even though I have a million questions about it.

"Hey," he says, then gestures towards our surroundings. "This is nice, huh?"

"You ain't seen nothing yet," I tell him with a knowing smile. "Wait 'til we get to the top."

"Oh yeah?" he grins. He pulls my hand up to his mouth and kisses it, and we tromp happily up the path, bathing in the evening sunlight as the kids run around us and laugh excitedly.

He can see over the summit a couple of steps before I can, and I hear him gasp.

"Oh, wow," he says.

"It's pretty special, huh?" I grin as we reach the top.

The view is spectacular. The other side of the hill dips down into a deep valley, where the river glistens blue and gold as it wends lazily around a series of huge boulders on either side. The steep inclines are full of evergreens on one side and fields on the other, and the sun is suspended in the v-shape between the mountains on the far side of the valley, painting the sky in vibrant shades of orange and pink as it sets.

"Stunning," I hear Ethan say across the way. He pulls Emily toward him and wraps his arms around her. I understand the impulse—it's a pretty romantic setting. And then I feel Greyson's arms wrap around me as he pulls me into the same embrace. It feels warm and safe, and I could stay here forever.

We all stand there a while, soothed into silence by the beauty of the scene before us. And then Sam clears his throat.

When I look over I can see him unlinking his arm from Drew's. He still doesn't look himself. The nervous energy that's been running through him all day has appeared on his face, and he licks his lips like his mouth is dry.

"What's up?" Drew asks him.

"Uh…" says Sam. He looks awkward for a moment, and then reaches into his pocket.

Sadie is the first one to gasp. I don't understand why until I see the little ring box in Sam's hand.

"Oh my God!" I whisper, nudging Greyson to get his attention.

The reaction of the adults silences the kids, and we all gather a little closer as Sam drops down to one knee on the summit.

"Andrew Archibald," he says, his voice a little shaky.

Greyson wraps his arm around me and tucks me into his side.

"I love you. Because you're kind and generous and smart. And I can't promise it'll be easy because, well… I'm not easy. But you're the first person I want to see in the morning, the first person I think of whenever something special happens, and possibly the only person who'd put up with me anyway."

We all laugh at that, including Drew.

"And I want to grow old with you and share a glass for our dentures."

Even more laughter, and Leo pipes up: "Gross."

"So will you do me the honor of being my husband? Will you marry me?"

He pops the box open to reveal a white gold ring with a Celtic pattern running around it. It suits Drew, who's nearly the same height as Greyson and almost as broad.

Drew is smiling.

"Yes," he answers, simply, and Sam lets all his nervous energy out as a loud laugh.

"Thank God for that!" he chuckles, pushing the ring onto Drew's finger. Drew yanks Sam to his feet, then pulls him into a tight hug while the rest of us clap and fawn over them.

I'm delighted for them. Drew is so good for Sam, and they're so well suited that the idea of them not being together is just... strange. Making it official seems just right.

"They been together long?" Greyson asks.

"About four years," I say, nodding.

He squeezes me a little tighter and kisses the top of my head, and I lean back against him, enjoying the warmth of his body against mine.

"I'm thankful for you," he whispers, and my tummy flips over.

❄

After the obligatory ring inspection, we all watch the sun set below the far-off peaks, quiet but for the children's chatter, and then Eddie guides us back down to the house with a huge, bright flashlight. We have a few more drinks and play a few games of charades, and then it's time for everyone to head off.

Greyson steals me off to the side while Ethan and Emily, each carrying a sleeping child, say their goodbyes.

"Thanks for making this happen," he says, lifting my chin with his finger. Every time he does that I feel a thrum of lust between my thighs.

"Oh, it wasn't me, it was… it… w…"

I trail off as he leans down, and he silences me with his kiss, gently pressing his lips against mine and coaxing them apart. I know he has to go back with his brother and I know I have to go home with the kids, and I have definitely drawn a mental line in the sand where him staying over at my house with the girls is just not allowed. But good heavens, I want him. Every inch of my body is screaming at me to find a way to be with him again, naked and panting and sweaty, and it's betrayed in the way I'm slightly breathless when he pulls back from the kiss.

"It was you," he says. "And it was amazing."

I bite my bottom lip and give a little shrug, not knowing how to respond to the compliment. So I opt for changing the subject entirely.

"So you don't need me next week?" I ask.

"Well, I wouldn't say that," he grins, mischievously. "But we won't be able to work on the house. They're fitting the bathroom and some new utilities. It'll be too much of a mess for us to get anything else done."

"Yeah," I nod. And then, before I realize I'm doing it, something about the romance of Sam's proposal, or the amazing day we've had, or our families being together like this, makes me throw caution to the wind.

"I'm going to get a Christmas tree on Tuesday morning, while the girls are at school," I say.

His brows lift immediately.

"I could use—"

"Yes," he says.

I laugh. "You don't even know what I was going to say!"

"I don't care what you were going to say," he grins. "The answer is yes."

I laugh again, shaking my head. "Fine. Come by at nine sharp."

"Yes ma'am," he says, leaning down to kiss me quickly again.

The hallway is suddenly flooded with people, and we spend at least five minutes saying our goodbyes.

"It was so lovely to meet you, Allie," Emily says, leaning over to kiss my cheek with a sleeping Riley in her arms. "You must come and visit us some time."

"I… uh…"

"She will," Greyson cuts in, and ushers her toward the door. He turns and gives me one last peck before disappearing into the night.

I stand there for a long moment, in stunned silence. Am I reading too much into that? Was it just an attempt to rescue me from an awkward conversation and get Emily out the door? Or did Greyson really just say that he'd take me to see his family in the city, someday? Is he… imagining a future for us? One that extends beyond Sunrise Valley House?

I think back to that first day in the diner, with my face crammed against Bet's and Sam's in the porthole window of the kitchen door, giggling as we tried to catch a glimpse of the handsome new stranger in town, and it suddenly feels like a million years ago.

CHAPTER 16

Greyson

BANG BANG BANG BANG BANG.

It's never-ending. The workmen arrived yesterday to start the bathroom refit, and all they did all day was bang. It's 8:30 am Tuesday and they've been banging again since eight. I'm glad Ethan, Emily, and the kids got out of dodge on Sunday. This is enough to drive a person mad.

Not me, though. I'm not going to be here much longer, and the prospect of meeting Allie today has been enough to keep me sane. I pull on my coat and scarf, run my hand through my hair in the mirror, and grab my keys.

"BACK LATER!" I yell up the stairs.

There's a muffled response between bangs, and I take that as acknowledgment enough. I already told them I'd be going out today. I also told Ethan when he called. And Ben. And pretty much anyone else I've had contact with since Thanksgiving last week. I do *not* want any interruptions.

I'm trying to play it cool, and my conscience does occasionally give me a little prick and tell me to stop enjoying myself so much. But for now, it's nice to be swept up in the excitement of a new relationship. Spending time with her over Thanksgiving was great, and today will be the first time we've been together, just the two of us, since being snowed into the mansion.

By the time I pull up to Allie's house less than ten minutes later, I can feel the nervous energy starting to build up inside me at the prospect of seeing her. There's no answer at the door when I knock, so I head back to my car and lean against it with my hands in my pockets.

As I'm standing there, wondering what exactly the word "sharp" means in this town, I notice the curtains twitch in the house next door. I think nothing of it and pull out my phone, flicking through emails and trying to avoid even noticing Peterson's. He's the type to set up read notices—so he gets notified when you read the emails he sends you—and take umbrage when he doesn't get a call back within the hour. I should probably be taking him and his demands for a meeting more seriously, but he's such an unbelievable douchebag that it's hard to take him seriously at the best of times. And here in Sunrise Valley, it feels like I'm beyond his reach.

I glance up and the curtains twitch again. I can see an old lady's pinched frown just before the curtains fall, and then I almost jump out of my skin when there's a loud WHOOP WHOOP! from a police siren behind me. I spin around to see the officer getting out of the car and heading right for me.

"Officer," I say with a nod.

It's not until he lifts his head and I can see under the brim of his hat that I realize it's Eddie.

"Greyson," he says and holds out his hand. I shake it, giving him a smile paired with a confused frown.

"Hey! I didn't know you were a cop."

"Yup," he says, nodding toward the house where the curtains have been twitching. "Old Mrs. Lisham next door called and said there was a strange man hanging around Allie's place."

"Ah," I say, glancing that way.

Now that she's seen Eddie shake my hand in a friendly manner, she seems much more amiable. She waves through the window, and Eddie and I both lift our hands to wave back.

"Here to see Allie?" he asks.

"Yeah, I'm supposed to be helping her get a—"

"Christmas tree?" he cuts in. "Yeah, no way she'd ever leave it 'til after the first. It's—"

"Tradition?" I cut back in.

Eddie grins back at me. "You're a fast learner."

"Morning, Eddie!"

I turn around to see the woman from next door is in her yard, wearing a long, quilted robe and curlers in her hair.

"Morning, Mrs. Lisham," says Eddie with a nod. "This is Greyson. A friend of Allie's."

"Oh," she says, smiling at me. "Oh, I see. Well, I'm sorry to have bothered you. You can't be too careful though!"

"That's right, Mrs. Lisham," says Eddie, indulgently. "You go on inside now before you catch yourself a cold."

"All right," she says. "Thanks, Eddie."

"Always here for you, Mrs. Lisham," says Eddie.

As soon as she closes the door, he turns to me and lowers his voice.

"Last time there was a burglary in this town was two years ago. The way Mrs. Lisham goes on, you'd think we were living in a game of GTA."

I laugh. That took me a little by surprise—Eddie doesn't seem like the gamer type.

"So Allie's not here," I say, a statement more than a question.

"She will be," he says, heading back to his car. "She's dropping the girls at school."

"Ahhhhh," I say, as it dawns on me. She said we'd be going to pick up the tree while the girls were at school. She must just be running late.

"See you 'round, Greyson," he calls with a wave, as he gets back into his car.

He's barely out of sight before I hear a couple of beeps, and Allie's car pulls into view.

"Hey!" she says as she gets out. She leans up to kiss me, and just as I bend down to wrap my arm around her waist and kiss her properly, I notice Mrs. Lisham's curtain twitching again.

"Hey," I say as I pull back to get a good look at her. "I just got in trouble with the law."

She laughs and jabs a thumb over her shoulder.

"I saw Eddie on the way in. Was he here for you?" She fixes me with a dark look. "Were you up to no good?"

"Yeah," I say, laughing. "Mrs. Lisham told him a suspicious man was skulking around your house." I give her a dark look of my own. "Are you aware, Ms. Brooks, that you're being stalked by a mysterious and irresistible stranger?"

She laughs a beautiful, amused laugh. "Mrs. Lisham would call Eddie if the leaves were rustling too loud," she says. "But sure, if it makes you happy. You're very mysterious and sexy."

She pats me on the shoulder, an expression of mock-encouragement on her face, and I find myself wanting to just pick her up, sling her over my shoulder, and carry her inside like some sort of caveman. Me man. She woman.

"Want to take my car?" she asks, oblivious to my Neanderthal daydreams. "You'll get pine needles all over your rental otherwise."

"Okay," I nod. I hit the button on my keychain to lock my car, and we walk over to hers

"Oh," she says. "You'll have to get in this side. That door doesn't work."

I look down at the passenger-side door and pull the handle, like I'm expecting it to open despite what Allie has just told me, and of course, it doesn't budge.

"You can climb through from the back if you'd prefer," she says, and when I look over she's wearing a sarcastic little smile.

I head around to the driver's side, leaning down to steal a quick kiss on the way, and then with great difficulty, I manage to maneuver my limbs inside her tiny car until I'm tucked into the passenger seat like a trussed turkey.

Allie gets into the driver's seat, looks over at me, and immediately lets out a burst of laughter.

"*Move the seat back*," she says like I'm an idiot.

"We should take my rental," I tell her grumpily.

"Needles," she reminds me. "And besides," she goes on with a twinkle in her eye. "You're stuck, now, sexy mystery man." She grins wickedly and turns the key to start the car.

It's a short trip to the tree farm, but by the time we get there I feel like I've been stuck in a trash compactor. I crawl out of the car like the girl from *The Ring* and stretch myself out with my hands on the back of my hips like an eighty-year-old. Allie, meanwhile, is collapsing in giggles.

"It's not funny," I say.

"It's quite funny," she replies, and she practically skips along in front of me to the front desk.

"Now, we need to be pretty fast," she continues. "Sadie's picking the girls up from school, but she'll be dropping them home at around noon."

I glance at my watch and it's 9:30. That means that it took 30 minutes to get here. The faster I get the tree in the car, the faster we get back to Allie's house and the more time we have. Alone.

I can feel my heart quicken at the very prospect of what I could do with an hour alone with Alora Brooks.

"Thank you," I say, interrupting the attendant who's giving us instructions about how we select and cut our tree. He pauses mid-sentence and Allie looks up to me with a puzzled expression, which only intensifies when I take her hand and pull her into the back lot, grabbing a saw on the way.

"Hey!" she says, "What's the rush?"

I come to a halt and turn to face her.

"Allie," I say, wearing my most serious face. "If we get this tree in, say, twenty minutes, get in the car, and drive back to your house, we'll have one hundred minutes."

She frowns and her eyes go up like she's doing the calculation herself.

"Together," I say.

"Uh,"

"Alone."

"Oh. *Oh!*" she says, as realization dawns.

Her face changes suddenly, sets with determination, and she grabs the saw out of my hand.

"Well come on," she says, as she starts stomping up the hill. "What are you waiting for?"

Good lord in heaven above, what did I do to deserve this woman? A broad grin appears on my face and I jog a few steps to catch up to her.

"Do you have any idea what I could do to you in one hundred whole minutes?" I ask.

Her cheeks start to flush, and I'm all in.

"You know, I really love the way your nipples feel on my tongue."

She gets a little redder, glances at me with her bottom lip tucked between her teeth.

"The way you taste…" I go on, and she lets out a little puff of air like a tiny bull about to charge.

"The way it feels when I'm inside you and you wrap your legs around my waist…"

"We can't go home without a tree," she says, as though she's trying to convince herself.

"They did have pre-cut, pre-packed trees in the foyer," I note, wearing my most innocent face.

She immediately tosses the saw in the grass, spins on her heels and grabs my hand, tugging me back down the hill, still wearing that very determined expression.

I'm grinning like a Cheshire cat the whole way down to the reception area. We grab a tree, already netted and tied, and Allie loads it into the trunk while I pay the very confused attendant.

"Get in," she practically snarls, standing by the open driver-side door, and pointing at it with her finger like some impatient schoolmarm.

I oblige, jamming my limbs back into the tiny car as best I can, and she jumps in and revs the engine.

She barely speaks all the way home. I glance at her a couple of times, but her eyes are fixed on the road and she's gripping the steering wheel so tight I'm half-convinced it'll snap off. She *looks* horny. It's something in her eyes, in the way she keeps shifting in her seat, the way she keeps swallowing… and how quiet she is.

When we arrive, she doesn't even attempt to get the tree out of the trunk. By the time I manage to unfold myself out of the car across the driver's seat, she's already inside the house, and she's left the door wide open.

I close the car door and walk up to the house at a leisurely pace, making a show of taking my time, teasing her. But as soon as I walk through the door she jumps on me.

She slams the door behind me, so hard that it shakes the chandelier in the hallway. Her lips are hungry on mine, her fingers are working at the buttons of my coat, and she moans quietly between kisses. I'm instantly, almost painfully hard.

"Allie, I…"

"Shh," she says, peeling my coat off my shoulders.

Part of me wants to pick her up and carry her off to the bedroom. But another part of me, more egotistical, more curious, wants to see how this frenzy she's worked herself into plays out. What exactly has she been thinking of, all the way home, while her knuckles turned white on the steering wheel?

Her fingers move to the bottom of my sweater and pull it up, and then her trembling hands start to fumble almost desperately with the button of my jeans.

My hardness is straining in my pants, and a ferocious, carnal need is building rapidly in my belly. I've never felt more wanted by a woman in my life. I barely have time to register the "zzzzip!" of my fly before she grabs my pants at the thighs and yanks them down.

And then Alora Brooks is in front of me, on her knees, and I'm pretty sure I could die happy right at this very moment. She pulls my underwear down, and I watch my length spring free of them and settle right in front of her beautiful face. She's in such a rush—no, a *hunger*—that she still has her coat and hat on, and somehow that makes her even sexier.

"Oh my *fucking God*," I groan, out loud, as she takes me into her mouth.

Nothing has ever felt so good as Allie's mouth engulfing my hardness. Nothing. She pulls back, applying just a little sucking pressure, and I groan as my head tilts upwards in appreciation. She places her hands on my thighs and starts to move back and forth in a slow, teasing rhythm, and the sheer pleasure of it makes me let out a loud, satisfied sigh.

"Holy shit, you're amazing," I breathe.

She keeps going, taking me deeper every time she pushes forward until I can feel my head slotting neatly into the back of her throat every time. She goes too deep and pulls back with a little cough. When I place a concerned hand on the side of her head, she bats it away and looks up at me.

I almost explode on the spot. Her lips are red and full, and she has just the tiniest hint of wet glistening in her eyes. There's a thin string of moisture still connecting her mouth to my length, and a shudder runs through my entire body.

Her look is a warning one. It tells me to let her do her thing, and I am more than happy to comply. She engulfs me again, her rhythm faster now, and I feel myself move closer and closer to the edge.

"Allie," I warn her, a rasp in my voice. "I'm going to come soon..."

She nods with my length in her mouth, and it slowly dawns on me that she has no intention of pulling away. A flash of what that's going to look like passes through my mind, and suddenly the orgasm that was approaching too quickly can't come soon enough. My hips twitch forward, again and again, as every pass of her tongue gets more sensitive. Finally, with my hands on either side of her head, I pull her onto me deeper, one last time, and tip over the edge, filling her mouth as I let out a deep, guttural, primal groan.

She pulls back and looks me straight in the eye as she swallows, and I swear to God I almost come again on the spot. She flicks the end of my head playfully, and I flinch and laugh, stepping back from her.

She's smiling, with her makeup smudged around her eyes and her lips still wet, and her stupid hat still on her head, and I know that I'm in trouble.

Actually, it's worse than that.

I'm in love.

CHAPTER 17

Allie

I don't know what came over me. I've *never* felt sheer, unadulterated need like that before, and if you told me a month ago that today I'd be doing what I just did to Greyson, I probably would've slapped you in the face. But here I am, still on my knees, trying to catch my breath, when Greyson suddenly pulls me to my feet and kisses me. And then, with a dangerous, animal look in his eyes, he throws me down onto the couch and pulls off my clothes with enough fervor you'd swear it was life or death.

By the time his fingers and his tongue have finished "repaying" me, my mind is blown, my head is swimming, and I'm in no state to do anything energetic for a while. So here we are, entangled on the sofa, half-naked, drinking fizzy water and sharing a pack of chips for brunch. It's very classy.

We chat, and laugh, and nuzzle into each other, and occasionally kiss, and it's really, really wonderful until my gaze passes across the clock above the fireplace and—

"SHIT!" I shout, jumping up from the couch. I grab my underwear and pants from the floor and start pulling them on. While I'm still hopping on one leg with the other in my jeans, I grab Greyson's sweater and throw it at him.

"Get dressed!" I say, although it's teetering on the brink of a scream. "Sadie will be here with the girls any minute!"

He grins at me lazily while he pulls on his sweater, and then stretches like a satisfied cat as he watches me frantically hop about, trying to pull on my jeans and boots and top at the same time.

"I guess I'd better get the tree, then," he says, maddeningly nonchalant, as he gets to his feet and pulls on his pants. He ambles over to me and leans down for a kiss, then saunters into the hallway and out to the car. I've never seen anyone so relaxed—let alone Greyson. I guess blowjobs really are like Xanax for men.

We just about manage to get the tree through the door and cut the netting away before the girls burst in.

"Mommy!" they shout, as they run through the door and into my arms. You can always trust kids to treat you the same way every day that a long lost friend would after a decade.

"Hey!" I say, crouching down to grab them both into hugs. "How was school?"

"I made paints!" says Emma, grinning from ear to ear.

"She did! Here it is," says Sadie, and holds up the painting. There's a large brown splodge in the middle that is clearly the result of a lot of paint being haphazardly slathered onto the same spot, with a few small streaks of the many colors that went into it still visible around the edges.

"Wow, look at you, my little Picasso!" I say, and Emma grins delightedly, despite not having the first clue who or what Picasso is.

"And how about you, Lottie?"

"We made Santas," she says. "With cotton balls and glitter and plates. But they have to dry before we can bring them home."

"Well, that sounds like fun," I say, leaning in to kiss her chilly little cheek.

As I stand up, I catch Sadie and Greyson exchanging quiet greetings out of the corner of my eye. I figure I'd better reintroduce the girls to him. It's been days since they saw him, which is practically decades in kid-years.

"Girls, you remember Greyson?"

"Yes. Hello!" says Lottie. At that precise moment, she notices the tree behind him, and Greyson is suddenly invisible as a little gasp comes out of her mouth.

"Treeeee!" she exclaims, looking up at me. She's one big grin in a little dress. "Teeeeeeee!" gasps Emma, following her sister's lead, and before we know it they're both jumping up and down and clapping maniacally.

"Are you helping us decorate it, Greyson?" Lottie asks.

He glances at me without answering, and I like the fact that he didn't automatically assume he'd be staying. However I feel about him, however much I lay awake at night, tossing and turning and trying to tell myself that I absolutely, positively cannot fall in love with a man who lives in New York City, there is still a line. I can be as foolish as I want with my own heart, but I will not risk the hearts of the two little girls who look to me to protect them.

"Sure?" I say with a shrug, trying to sound casual. "If you want. You can have dinner with us." I pause for a beat. "Before you go home later."

Oh very smooth, Allie. Definitely not cringing internally at the way I crowbarred that last bit in. But as awkward as it came out, it needed to be said.

Greyson doesn't seem bothered at all. Instead, he just shouts "Yaaay!" in unison with the girls, then listens very, very intently as they explain exactly how we're going to decorate the tree. *Good Lord, he's a dork!* Did not see that coming, the first few weeks he was here. But it's absolutely charming.

I walk Sadie to the door. "Thanks for taking them today," I say quietly. "It was a big help."

"You're welcome. I heard you had a home invader this morning." She nods to Greyson.

"Ugh, Mrs. Lisham," I say, rolling my eyes. "I suppose it's nice that she looks out for me."

"Yeah," says Sadie, stepping through the door. "So... he came to get the tree with you?" Her face is a picture of innocence, and yet it also manages to convey that she knows something's up.

"Mmhmm," I say, shrugging one shoulder.

"Isn't that one of the pre-packed trees they sell at the front door?"

"Bye Sadie," I say, smiling broadly as I close the door.

By the time I get back inside, the girls have each taken one of Greyson's hands and are pulling him up the stairs, excitedly telling him that Lottie knows where I keep all the decorations. This is not true, and I suspect that the girls are trying to rope Greyson into a scavenger hunt with them. Quickly deciding that I'd prefer not to have Greyson wandering around upstairs in case he sees anything too embarrassing in, say, for instance, the second drawer of the nightstand beside my bed, I run up after them and steer them towards the loft. A little while later, the tree is propped up on its stand and we're all happily singing along to Christmas music and hanging baubles wherever we can reach.

There is one particular branch at the bottom of the tree that Emma seems to favor, it being one of the few she can actually reach, and it sags with the weight of all the shiny balls she's hung on it.

"Wow!" says Greyson. "Look at that! That's the coolest branch ever!"

"What about this one?" asks Lottie, pointing at one of the ones she's been decorating.

Greyson doesn't say "oh, shit!" out loud, but it flashes across his face for a moment. He quickly replaces it with an expression of feigned shock.

"Holy smokes!" he says. "I didn't see that one! I can't believe we have two branches that are exactly as beautiful as each other on the same tree!"

I laugh and shake my head, and when the girls are distracted again he looks over at me, puffs out his cheeks, and wipes his arm across his brow in a "phew!" motion.

We finish off the tree with some tinsel and stand back to admire our handiwork.

"It's so pretty," says Lottie, wistfully.

"Pitty," agrees Emma, standing beside her.

"Mommy." Lottie looks up at me with her big blue eyes, the spitting image of Libby. "Can we put Heaven Mommy and Daddy on now?"

I lean down and squeeze her, nodding. "Of course, sweetheart," I say, and reach into the decorations box to pull out another, smaller box from inside. I sit on the floor and the girls gather in beside me, one on either side, and though he remains standing I can tell that Greyson is watching intently, letting us have our moment.

Inside the box is a beautiful, angel-shaped tree topper, glittering silver, and at the top of each wing is a tiny photo frame. Libby's picture is on one side and Alex's picture is on the other side.

Emma doesn't understand. She doesn't remember. But Lottie reaches her little hand out and runs her fingertip gently over each of their faces, then looks up to me and smiles. It's easier this year than it was last year or the year before, but it still takes every ounce of strength I have to hold back the tears and be strong for them.

"Heaven Mommy was really pretty," Lottie says. I nod, looking at my sister's smiling face in the photo and wishing with my whole heart that I could hear her laugh just one more time.

"She was, darling. The most pretty girl in all the world, until you were born." I kiss the top of her head. "Shall we put it up?"

Lottie nods and takes the angel from me. And then she looks up to Greyson.

"Will you pick me up?" she asks.

One look at him and I can tell that her innocent little face has absolutely crushed him. There are no tears in his eyes, but I see a tidal swell of emotion pass across his face for a split second before he gathers himself into a wide smile and nods.

"It would be my honor to do such an important job," he says, his voice cracking just a little before he regains control. He takes her gently by the waist and lifts her up until she can reach the treetop. Emma hugs my leg, watching.

Lottie places the angel very carefully, like it's the most precious thing in the world, then pulls her little hands back into her chest and stares up at it for a moment.

"It's perfect," Greyson whispers.

"Yeah," Lottie nods. "Perfect."

❄

We let Greyson do the honor of switching on the lights, since he's the guest, and there's great excitement as the tree comes alive in a swarm of flashing, multicolor strobes. The girls cheer and dance around the living room, and Greyson gives me an affectionate squeeze as we watch them.

"Greyson! Greyson!" Lottie comes running over to us. "Are you coming to the Christmas fair?"

He looks at me, brows raised questioningly.

"It's on Thursday," I say. "There are Christmas stalls and games. And Santa comes to visit."

"Mommy gets special elf powers for the day," Lottie whispers to him.

"I do," I say, nodding solemnly. "Santa's real elves are all busy at the workshop making toys, so Santa sprinkles a little magic dust on me and gives me elf powers for the day so I can help him when he comes to Sunrise Valley to see all the children."

Greyson grins, no doubt amused at the thought of me in an elf costume. Well, the joke's on him—I love it. I'm the best elf this side of The North Pole.

"Well, I…" he says. He looks at me again, like he's holding out for my permission to accept Lottie's invitation.

"You should come," I say, nodding. "If you want."

"Santa is bringing presents for me," says Emma.

"Well you're very lucky," Greyson tells her. He turns to Lottie. "And I'd love to come."

"Wear your best Christmas sweater!" I grin.

He shakes his head emphatically.

"Nope! I don't wear Christmas sweaters. Or hats. That's where I draw the line."

"Scrooge," I tease.

He laughs, but I can tell he's not joking.

CHAPTER 18

Greyson

I can't believe I'm doing this.

It's not that I hate Christmas. I'm just not into it the way some people are, you know? Ethan always wears the stupid sweaters and Santa hats, he's the first to put the decorations up, he switches the music in his car to Christmas tunes in the middle of November. He's always loved it, and if he were given the opportunity to play Santa for an entire town of kids, he'd probably jump at the chance. But that's not me.

And yet here I am, buttoning up a velvety red coat and adjusting my ridiculous fake beard in the mirror, all because a pretty girl with beautiful eyes stomped her little foot at me. God, I'm a sucker.

I'd only just arrived at the Christmas fair in my decidedly not-Christmassy garb, looking forward to an evening of occasionally dipping my head into Santa's grotto to laugh at Allie the elf, when I spotted her in deep conversation with Bet behind one of the tents.

"There you are!" I said, walking up to them, not yet realizing what I was in for.

Have you ever watched—actually seen the moment—when a plan hatches itself in someone's mind, and you can see it on their face? I have. I saw it right there, in Ally's eyes, as she saw me approaching.

"Greyson!" she half-shouted at me, "How would you like to be our Santa?"

"Uh…" Like a hole in the head? Like a fish needs a bicycle? "No thanks."

"The thing is, dear," said Bet, all consoling sweetness. "I went to fetch Robert Miller, who was…" she paused and looked around, then lowered her voice to a hissed whisper in case there were any children in earshot. "… supposed to be our Santa. But he forgot the fair was today. And he spent the afternoon at Christmas drinks with work. And… well, he's in no fit state to be Santa, that's for sure."

"No," I replied, shaking my head resolutely. "No no no no no. No way."

"You *have* to do it," Allie chimed in. "The suit's so big it would drown Sam, and Drew is working the Pin the Tail on the Turkey booth. There's nobody else."

"I am *not* doing it!" I replied, folding my arms as though that were the end of the matter.

And then, finally realizing that I genuinely, absolutely had no intention of doing it, Allie pulled out the big guns. She *batted her eyelids at me.* Her big, green eyes looked up at me, pleadingly, and—oh my God, there was even the hint of a tear forming in one of them.

"Please, Greyson? It would mean so much to the kids... to Lottie and Emma..."

God. Dammit.

And that's how I ended up here, pulling on a pair of black boots with a trim of fake snow at the top, and adjusting the big fake belly that came with the costume underneath my thick red coat.

"How's it going?" calls Allie from outside. "The kids will be here soon."

I pull open the curtain and glare down at her.

She has the good grace not to laugh, but she can only pull it off by sucking her twitching lips in between her teeth.

"You look great," she says. She leans up, the bell on the end of her little elf hat jingling as she does, and kisses me on the cheek. "Thank you."

"You'd better make it worth my while," I gruff.

She tries to give me a saucy wink, but it looks comical with her outfit and the red circles painted on her cheeks. It brings a smile to my face, at least.

"Now, listen," she says, looking suddenly very serious. "These kids believe you are Santa. They truly, really, with every bit of their heart believe it. So you have to go along with them. Some of them will ask for crazy things and some of them might ask for sad things, and you might have to get a little bit creative with what you tell them because all we're giving out today are candy canes, toy cars, and dolls, but just... stay in the fantasy with them."

Seeing how seriously she takes it makes me realize, putting aside my own embarrassment for the first time, the gravity of the responsibility that's been landed in my lap. I nod solemnly back to her.

"Don't worry, Allie," I say, sounding at least twice as confident as I feel. "I've got this."

"Great!" she says, her face brightening into a grin. "Your chair is over there," she says. "I'll get the first kid."

She half turns away, then turns back. "Oh, and don't worry if any of them pee on you. We have spare pants."

"Wha—"

Before I can express my horror at the prospect of being peed on by an excited child, she's disappeared through the grotto curtain. I take my seat, unsure of what to expect next.

Less than half a minute later, the curtain pulls back again and Allie re-enters the grotto, leading a chubby boy of about five by the hand.

"This is Elijah," she says, and the boy skips across the room, beaming, and plants himself happily in my lap.

❄

Most of the kids ask for the same sorts of things. Remote toy cars, talking dolls, video games, that kind of thing. Occasionally there'll be a more exotic request—one kid asks for a real, live T-Rex. I manage to handle most of them with aplomb, even if I do say so myself. The T-Rex kid is very understanding of the fact that dinosaurs need a lot of sleep and won't fit on human beds.

"That was great," Allie says, smiling at me. "You're a natural."

Her praise makes my chest puff out, and I pull the next kid up onto my lap with way more enthusiasm.

"Ho, ho, ho!" I say. "Merry Christmas! What's your name, little girl?"

"Isabella," she says. She's wearing a pink princess dress and her hair is up in neat twin braids. She has a headband full of purple stars with a unicorn horn sticking up from the middle of it.

"And what do you want for Christmas, Isabella?" I ask this perfectly sweet little girl.

"A crowbar," she says.

I nearly choke with laughter. I cover it with a cough, and when I glance up her mother is standing behind her, waving her hands back and forth across each other and mouthing "NO!" at me.

"Well," I say carefully. "The thing is, the elves need all the crowbars to open the boxes and boxes full of toys that come in for boys and girls all over the world. If we start giving them away, we won't be able to sort the toys and get them all packed up, will we?"

Isabella looks up at me thoughtfully. Before she opens her mouth, I can tell she's skeptical.

"But if all the boxes are already open by Christmas night," she says, "won't you be able to send me one then, because you won't need them anymore?"

Smart kid.

"But what will we do next year?" I ask.

She purses her lips. "Well. They sell them in Lowe's," she says. "You could get another one by next year."

Behind her, her mother claps a hand to her own forehead.

I'm having a hard time keeping a straight face. Thank God for the beard. I nod very seriously and rack my brains for a response that will save Isabella's poor, haggard-looking mother from having to gift her daughter a crowbar come Christmas morning.

"Well it's not that simple, Isabella," I say. "You see, the crowbars I have at my workshop are magical ones. Irreplaceable. If I start giving them away, we'll be short. The elves might not get everyone's presents ready in time for me to deliver them."

Isabella is satisfied with this. She shrugs like it's no big deal.

"Okay. Well, then I'd like a unicorn lamp for my bedroom," she says.

Isabella's mother presses the palms of her hands together and mouths "thank you," to me.

"That was a close one," I say to Allie, as Isabella skips out of the grotto, holding her mother's hand.

"You're doing great," says Allie. "Emma's up next, then Lottie."

"Oh!" I say, a big smile stretching across my face. I'm delighted that Allie's girls are coming in. A ripple of excitement rolls through me, and I rearrange my beard and hat in preparation.

"Ho, ho, ho!" I say, as Emma sprints over and wriggles herself up onto my lap. "Merry Christmas, Emma."

She grins up at me.

"What do you want for Christmas?"

"Uhhh," she says, tapping her chin and looking deeply thoughtful. "Pony toy," she says. "And a hot dog."

I glance up at Allie who rolls her eyes, smiling, and gives me a shrug.

"I think I can deliver on the pony toy," I say. "But your aunt Sadie is in charge of Christmas dinner."

Emma is satisfied with our negotiations and goes skipping off out of the Grotto. Bet is just outside the exit, handing out gifts as the children leave.

"Hello, Santa," says Lottie, as I turn back towards the entrance.

"Oh!" I cry, "—ho-ho!" Not a bad recovery, if I say so myself. I hadn't expected her to be there so quickly.

"Hello, Lottie," I say, my voice deep.

She looks very serious as she gets into my lap and settles her hands on her own knees.

I look up to Allie, questioningly, and she shrugs.

"Have you been good this year?" I ask.

"Yes, I think so," she says, pensively. "I've been mean to my little sister a couple of times, but I never meant it and I always said sorry."

"Mmm," I nod. "Yes, I remember. I think you've done a good job, overall."

"Thank you, Santa," she says, matter-of-factly accepting the compliment.

"And what do you want for Christmas?" I ask.

"Well," she says. "I don't really want any toys. I have lots of those. And Emma—that's my sister—breaks lots of my stuff anyway. And I don't want food because Mommy always gives me food and I think you should probably deliver all the food to the people who don't have any."

I nod. The wisdom of children.

"So then what do you want?" I ask.

She glances at Allie, then shifts on my lap and leans up to whisper quietly in my ear.

"I want Mommy to keep smiling the way she has been lately," she says, and I am suddenly, ferociously uncomfortable.

It's like I've been teetering near this line I was never supposed to cross, and now I've tripped and fallen over it. And the prospect of hurting good, innocent people, *again*, is looming like the ghost of Christmas past. The grotto walls feel like they're closing in on me as Lottie jumps down from my lap and walks toward the exit.

"Oh, and Santa," says Lottie. "I would also like for Mommy's friend Greyson to come to my school play."

She heads out through the curtain, and I sit there with my chest feeling tight and my heart feeling heavy, trying to snap myself out of it.

"What did she ask for?" asks Allie, looking at me with concern.

"Oh," I say, forcing a fake brightness into my voice. "It's a secret," I tell her, pushing a smile up behind the mask.

Allie looks at me, a little puzzled, but before she can press the matter Sadie's three-year-old, Finn, comes marching in. With some difficulty, I manage to push the discomfort out of my mind. There's still a lot of kids to go, and they didn't come here to see a morose Santa in the middle of an existential crisis.

It takes a couple of hours to get through all the children. By the time I've "ho'd" my last "ho" and changed out of my Santa costume, I'm feeling (and looking) more like myself.

"I heard Santa was a hit!" says Sam, coming over to meet us as Allie and I emerge from the back of the grotto. He's carrying a clipboard and wearing a broad smile.

"Yes he was!" says Allie, grabbing around my arm. "He was brilliant."

She looks up to me with a doting grin, and I suddenly feel like a superhero. It still amazes me, how her smallest glance can make me feel.

"Greyson! Greyson!" Lottie is calling. She's running across the field with a stick of cotton candy in her hand.

"Hey, Lottie," I say, smiling as she stops beside us. "Are you enjoying the fair?"

"Yeah, it's great!" she says. "Santa said he'd make you come to my school play!"

I glance at Allie, who's looking up at me hopefully, and once again I feel the crushing weight of expectations I'm sure I can't meet. But I can't say no.

"Well then," I say, reaching down to flick a bit of cotton candy from her nose. "I guess I'll be going to your school play!"

Lottie positively beams up at me and gives a little cheer. "River!" she calls, turning around to run back over to her cousin. "River! Santa made it come true!"

"It's on Thursday afternoon next week," says Allie. "Emma's pre-school is doing a little play the same day, just before Lottie's. But it's okay if you can't make it, I'll just tell her something came up."

"No," I say. "No, I'll be there. For both of them."

CHAPTER 19

Allie

There's something off about Greyson today. It's the morning of the girls' school plays, and since the bathroom fitters have finished up and left, I've come to help tidy up the mess of sawdust and plastic wrap they left behind.

I've barely seen him since the fair, despite inviting him over a couple of times for dinner. I can't help but wonder if he, like me, is starting to realize that Christmas is fast approaching. In two weeks it'll be upon us, and he'll be done with Sunrise Valley House. And then what?

"Everything all right?" I ask him, entering the kitchen to take a break and make a coffee.

He's been sitting at the breakfast bar all morning, clacking away on his keyboard.

"Hmm?" he says, looking up. "Oh. Yeah. Great."

He gives me a tight smile and looks back to his screen, and I frown and turn around to fill the coffee machine.

"Coffee?" I ask.

"Thanks," he replies, shortly.

I brew the coffee in silence, becoming more and more irritated until I give myself a talking to and remind myself that he's actually a very busy guy. He's probably finishing up some work so he can come along to the girls' school plays later.

"Here you go," I say, placing a steaming mug down in front of him. He looks at it with a confused expression, like he doesn't remember asking for it. But then his face clears, and he looks up to me and smiles, more like the Greyson I've come to know and less like the one that arrived in Sunrise Valley a month ago.

God. Has it only been a month? It feels like I've known him forever. It feels like he's a part of my life now, despite the fact that we haven't talked about our relationship or the fact that he's supposed to be leaving in a couple of weeks. Every time I think about it, I push the thought out of my mind. I'm guessing he does the same.

And considering all that, I've begun to think that I may have bent my cardinal rule to the breaking point: I've let him get too close to the girls. Lottie's little face lit up when he said he was coming to the play, and while I'm glad she likes him, I know I've messed up. Because we haven't had the talk about what will happen between us when it's time for him to go, and because Lottie and Emma have already known enough loss in their short little lives.

"Are you okay?" Greyson asks. I must have been letting all that worry play out on my face because he looks concerned.

"Hmm?" I say, buying some time. "Oh. Yeah. Just trying to remember if I packed the girls' costumes into their bags this morning."

"Ah," says Greyson. "I bet they're excited."

"They were bouncing," I say. I smile, but I know it doesn't have the usual sparkle. It feels like we've both jumped at this chance to talk about the kids because it's simple and pleasant. And because it avoids everything painful and complicated that we should be talking about instead.

"So what are they going to be?" he asks, picking up his coffee and giving me his full attention.

"Well," I say, "Emma is a cloud."

"A cloud?"

"Yeah. It's preschool. They just dress up and sing some cute Christmas songs. It'll be over in about a half-hour. Three-year-olds don't have very good attention spans."

"Fair point," he grins.

"And Lottie is the star."

"*The* star?" he asks.

I smile proudly, puffing like a preening mother goose. "Yup!" I say. "*The* star, guiding the wise men. She has a solo. She's super excited."

"Wow," says Greyson. "That's pretty impressive. She's a special kid."

I nod at that, feeling a swell of pride.

"Yeah," I say. "She really is. She—"

I cut off when Greyson's phone starts ringing and he immediately picks it up from the table.

"Sorry," he says, lifting it up and setting his coffee down. "I really have to take this."

He pushes up from his stool and heads out of the room.

"Ben," I hear him say as he heads through the door, pressing his phone to his ear. "Hit me."

I stand in the kitchen alone and let out a sigh, sipping my coffee again.

Is this what it's like when he's working, I wonder? Is he always so distracted and put-upon and worried-looking? And does it even matter, if he's leaving in a couple of weeks and I'm staying here?

I wish I had been able to tuck my heart away in a little box and care for it the way I should have, but the truth is that I pulled it out and handed it to him that day we kissed in the mud. And now I fear he may be about to skip town without giving it back.

I pour both our coffees down the sink and head back upstairs, put my headphones on, and set my playlist on loud to try and drown out my own thoughts.

I don't come back downstairs until it's time to leave. Greyson is sitting on the same seat in the kitchen, tapping away on his laptop, as though not a moment has passed. I feel another irrational spike of irritation rising in my gut.

"Ready?" I ask.

He looks at me with a blank expression, then looks at his screen to see the time.

"Shit," he says with an irritated sigh. He shakes his head like a wet dog would, as though he's trying to clear his thoughts, then grabs his phone and stands up. "Yeah," he says. "Let's go."

I've half a mind to tell him it doesn't matter. That he can skip it if he has so much work to do. But it *does* matter. He promised Lottie.

He *promised*.

"I'm going to take off. Meet me on Main Street," I say, smiling at him quickly, and I head out of the door before my irritation can creep onto my face.

CHAPTER 20

Greyson

As soon as I get into the car outside the mansion, I notice that Ben has forwarded yet another message from Lincoln Fucking Peterson. Not his actual middle name, but it should be.

He's threatening all sorts of legal action if he doesn't have an in-person meeting with me immediately, like today. Except I'm hundreds of miles away, with no desire to see him. And judging by the way Allie's tires chewed up the gravel a minute ago when she left, she's pissed at me, too.

I drop my phone down onto the passenger seat and rub my temples, taking a deep breath and sighing it out. Then I put the rental into drive and head out onto the road.

In fairness to Peterson—not that he deserves any fairness—this mess is my fault. I've been ignoring his increasingly irate emails and messages since I arrived in Sunrise Valley. At first, it was because I know him, and he can usually be talked down by someone else before I actually have to get involved. And then it was because I didn't want to talk to the jackass and end up having to leave Allie and the girls just to sort out whatever trivial shit he's taking issue with.

As I pull into Main Street, my phone rings. It's Ben.

"Yeah?" I say abruptly when I hit the button to answer.

"Yeah, so Peterson's secretary called again. Said he's going to speak to his lawyer this afternoon if he doesn't see you."

"God, he's such a dick," I spit.

There's a pause before Ben starts to speak, very deliberately and carefully.

"No-one disagrees, Boss," he says. "But he's also our biggest client and he's been ramping up for a month. I offered him Cecie." That's our Chief Customer Officer. It's not her name. Her name is Victoria but we started calling her Cecie as a joke when she became CCO and it stuck. "I offered him Ethan. He's not interested."

He's right, of course. This is my mess now, and I need to clean it up.

I pull up behind Allie's car on Main Street. She's standing beside it, arms folded, looking a few shades less cheery than her usual self. She smiles at me, but she also lifts her phone up, facing me, and taps the large digital clock on the lock screen.

I glance at my car's clock and it's 1:55 pm. Emma's concert starts at two.

"All right, listen. I have to go to a thing right now. Keep me updated. I'll see what I can come up with."

"Greyson, I—"

I don't want to hear it. My stress levels are at maximum and I have an awful, foreboding feeling that everything is coming to a head. That no matter what I do, I'm going to let someone down. So I swipe my biggest problem away with my thumb, cut Ben off mid-sentence, and get out of the car.

"Ready?" says Allie.

I nod, shove my phone in my pocket, and walk into the hall beside her.

❅

"Welcome, welcome everyone!" says a shrill-voiced teacher, standing in front of a gaggle of over-excited toddlers. Emma is right at the front, encased in a big, white, puffy costume. She beams when she sees Allie and me, waving her little hand so fast it looks like a propellor. We both smile and wave back as we take our seats The murmur of conversation around the hall gradually gives way to a hushed silence, as proud-faced parents and grandparents all turn towards the stage to see their little angels—or clouds, as the case may be—sing.

I'm trying to put everything else out of my mind and give Emma my full attention, but it's proving more difficult than I thought. I'm not even aware that my leg is shaking until Allie reaches over and presses her hand on top of it.

"Thanks," I say, and she gives me a genuinely warm smile in return. I can't tell if she's less pissed at me, or just delighted to be here watching Emma's first school play.

"We wish you a Merry Christmas, we wish you a Merry Christmas," the kids start singing. It's completely out of tune, but they're certainly giving it their all. They've got a little dance to go with the song, and they're really getting into the choreography, their eyes glued to the teacher as they swing their arms from side to side like energetic little pirates. I can't help but smile at how positively wholesome this is. And then I feel my phone vibrate in my pocket, and it wipes the grin clean off my face.

It's an SMS message from Ben.

```
Ethan wants you to call him. Peterson on
warpath.
```

I clench my jaw and shove the phone back into my pocket. I have no idea how I'm going to get out of this without either blowing up my business, and therefore my brother's livelihood, or destroying whatever it is I have with Allie.

But isn't that on the verge of ending anyway? She's said she has no intention of ever leaving Sunrise Valley while the girls are still small, and my current predicament just goes to show that working remotely just isn't going to be an option for me.

My phone buzzes again and I pull it out. Another message from Ben.

```
He says ASAP
```

I clench my jaw again, so hard I think my teeth might crack, and then I feel the pressure of Allie squeezing my hand. Hard.

I look over to her and she's staring at me with wide eyes and a deeply unimpressed expression on her face. She directs a very exaggerated nod at my phone.

The pressure inside me is building so much I'm not sure I can take any more. I give her an apologetic smile and, in what can only be a moment of sheer madness, I press my phone's power button down hard enough to turn my fingertip white, and switch it off.

Allie smiles and squeezes my hand more gently this time, and we go back to watching the adorable, familiar little cloud in the front row.

❄

"Wow!" I say as Emma comes running over to us after the concert is done. "You were amazing! Star of the show!"

Allie gathers Emma up in her arms and pulls her into a tight hug, and we filter out of the hall with all the other parents.

"You know where Lottie's school is?" asks Allie, outside. "Just down the street from the church? Her play will be starting in about fifteen minutes."

"I know the one," I nod. "I'll meet you there."

As soon as I get into the car, I dig the phone out of my pocket and switch it on. A stream of messages comes in, each one more urgent than the last, and then it starts ringing in my hand.

Ethan.

Oh, shit.

"Hey," I say, as casually as I can.

"Don't you fucking 'hey' me!" he says. I can hear the stress in his voice, plain as day. "Where the hell are you? Peterson's lawyer just called legal."

"Fuck."

"Yeah, 'fuck' is right. I don't care what else you have going on over there, Greyson—call this jerk, find out what he wants and give it to him, or he's going to sue us into the ground because *you* didn't do your *fucking job*."

I swallow hard. This is… not like Ethan. He doesn't get angry, and he especially doesn't get angry with his kid brother.

"Okay," I say. I don't have any excuses for him, because every one of them sounds frivolous or stupid. "Okay. Sorry, Ethan."

"Don't apologize," he says, through what sounds like gritted teeth. "Fix it."

"I will," I say, and hang up. "Call Ben."

The phone doesn't even get through half a ring before he picks up.

"What can I do?" he asks, without missing a beat.

"Set up a meeting. Tomorrow. And get me a flight out of Plattsburgh today."

"Done," he says. "I'll send the details through."

"Thanks, Ben. Sorry about earlier."

"No worries, Boss," he says, and I hang up.

And then I grip the steering wheel in both hands and lean forward, pressing my head against it.

"FUCK!" I bellow.

I have to go back to the house and pack a bag. Right now, if Ben's record is anything to go by. He'll have me on a flight within two hours.

I'd be lying if I said there wasn't a part of me that just wants to drive straight back to the house and avoid telling Allie. But I have to face the music.

When I arrive at Lottie's school, Allie and Emma are waiting outside. There are only a couple of other people hurrying down the path, so it looks like I'm late. I get out of the car and jog across the road, stopping a few paces from her.

"Hey," she says, smiling. But her face drops as she notices the drawn expression on my own. "What's wrong?"

I gaze beyond her to the school hall. Lottie is probably rehearsing her big solo right now, buzzing with excitement. I desperately want to grant her Christmas wish—to walk into the hall, sit down right in the front row, give her a big thumbs-up during her solo, clap and cheer at the end—but it would mean potentially ruining my brother. And myself.

"I can't come," I say.

I can't even look at Allie. I hate myself so much I feel sick.

She doesn't respond. When I do finally muster the guts to look at her, her face is absolutely blank.

"I have to go back to the city. For a work thing. Urgently."

I know my eyes are pleading, but there's still nothing on her face

God, I wish she'd scream, or shout, or…

"Okay," she says, giving me a tight smile. "Well, I need to get inside."

She turns around with Emma in her arms, intent on making sure Lottie has someone there to see her—even if it's not the one person she explicitly asked for. Emma gives me a little wave over Allie's shoulder, and I loathe myself with every last ounce of feeling I have left.

My phone buzzes again and I pull it out of my pocket to see a message from Ethan.

```
Thanks, bro. I knew you'd fix it.
```

A lump rises in my throat, thick and heavy. I feel a sudden wave of revulsion for the phone and everything on the other end of it, and I shove it back into my pocket with such force that I hear the lining tear.

CHAPTER 21

Allie

I wake up groggy and dehydrated from crying myself to sleep last night. My eyes are puffy, my nose is red, and my face is blotchy all over.

"Mommy, you look sick!" says Lottie, diving under my covers. She was a little disappointed that Greyson couldn't make it to her show last night, but she was far too pleased with the standing ovation she got for her solo to let it bother her that much.

I don't know why I'm so upset. I knew it was coming. I knew he'd be leaving. And it's only happened two weeks earlier than I had thought it was.

Actually, I do know why I'm so upset. I feel stupid. And gullible. Stupid for letting him in, and gullible for believing that having his family over for Thanksgiving and decorating the tree together and inviting him to the fair would do anything but encourage the girls to get attached to him. In the back of my mind, I realize now, I was hoping that all of it might convince him to stick around. Last night was a rude awakening to reality.

"I'm all right, darling," I tell Lottie.

Emma stirs beside me, opening her sleepy little eyes. She wriggled into my bed at 3 am and hugged me tighter than she ever has before as she fell asleep. I think she knew I was sad, and that breaks my heart.

I would love to mope about here all day and cry into my pillow, but it's just not an option. I force a bright smile onto my face and sit up.

"Right!" I say. "Time to get ready for school. Who wants pancakes for breakfast as a special treat for doing so well in your concerts yesterday?"

"Yaaaaaay!"

The two of them are suddenly wide awake, and they run ahead of me down the stairs—Lottie reminding Emma to hold on tight to the banister. I gather my hair up into a bun, pull on some jeans and a hoodie, and tromp down the stairs to make their pancakes.

※

"Holy mother of God," says Sadie as I open the door. She's come to collect the kids, and I'm still in my unkempt jeans and hoodie with my face blotchy and swollen.

"Thanks," I croak.

"Are you sick?"

I shake my head. Sade glances at the girls, who are busy collecting up their coats and bags, and leans in towards me. "Greyson?" she whispers.

I give her a tight little smile and nod slightly.

"I'll come back when I've dropped the kids off," she says.

"No," I tell her, shaking my head. "I need to go collect my stuff from the mansion and leave the key. Might as well rip off the bandaid."

"Did you cut yourself, Mommy?" asks Lottie, overhearing.

"I'm fine, sweetheart," I call back.

"That bad, huh?" asks Sadie, keeping her voice low. The pity on her face is too much for me, and I have to look away before I burst into tears.

"You girls have a great day!" I chirp, far more brightly than I feel.

Sadie squeezes my arm and promises she'll stay awhile when she brings the kids back from school this afternoon. I smile back, hoping that it looks braver than I feel. I don't think I can hold it together much longer.

I close the door as soon as they're through it, just in time. A sob hiccups out of me, and I clamp my hand over my mouth to try and hold it in, only for another to come after it, and another, and another. Realizing that the battle is lost, I throw myself down on the couch and decide to just let myself cry until I don't need to anymore. My trip to the mansion can wait for another hour.

❄

Cucumbers are wonderful things. By the time I drive over to the mansion, my eyes are much less puffy, even if I still feel like shit.

I pull to a halt on the gravel driveway, not even bothering to go around the side of the house where the cars are normally parked. This won't take long.

I dig the old iron key out of my bag and slide it into the lock, just as I have so many times before. It turns with a loud clank, and I push the door open.

I stop dead in my tracks when I see Greyson standing in the hall. He has his coat on and his suitcase in his hand.

"Allie..." For a moment it looks like he's going to say something more. But the words seem to catch in his throat.

I look from him down to the case and back up.

"You're still here," I say, too astonished to say anything else.

"Ben couldn't get a flight 'til this morning."

I'm suddenly, utterly and unrelentingly furious.

"YOU'RE *STILL HERE!*" I practically spit at him. This time I can feel the anger crawling through my veins and onto my face. I can hear it in my own voice.

"I didn't know when the flight would be."

"You *promised* Lottie! *Promised* her! And then you let her down... *for nothing!*" I shout at him. "You're *still here!*"

Greyson looks like he's been punched in the gut.

"I'm sorry," he mumbles.

He doesn't even try to explain. He just stands there with his head down, staring at the floor, and I have never in my life wanted to smack someone so badly.

"Is that all you've got to say?" I demand, my shoulders lifting and falling with the heavy breaths I'm taking.

"You're better off without me," he says, looking away.

I let out a derisive little snort, half anger and half surprise.

"That old cliche? Give me a break, Greyson."

"What do you want me to say?" he asks.

What do I want him to say? The question pulls me up short. What *do* I want him to say? He hasn't broken any agreement —we never had one. He didn't keep his promise to Lottie, but if I'm honest, I'm more upset about that than she is. He's leaving a couple of weeks earlier than he was supposed to, that's all. So why do I feel so angry about it?

"Nothing," I snap, irritation and bile rising up behind my sternum. "Nothing at all. Go back to your life like you were always going to."

Ugh. Does that sound pathetic? Part of me thinks it sounds pathetic and I want to kick myself for being so vulnerable.

Greyson's nostrils are flared and his jaw is tensed. He looks upset and angry. *Good*. It's not a noble thought, but part of me likes the discomfort painted across his face. It matches the turmoil I feel inside myself.

For a moment, it looks like he's about to yell something back at me, and I find myself praying that he does. Because that would at least tell me that he's not completely at ease with the idea of breezing out of my life like I'm nothing to him and never was.

But he doesn't do that. He takes deep, long breaths until his jaw is relaxed and his expression is level, and he looks me right in the eye and says: "It's only two weeks."

Bubbling, rage-filled madness grips me and a loud, bitter laugh comes out of my mouth.

"You're right. You're right! What was I thinking? Two weeks! Why, that's almost a third of the time we've known each other!" I scoff, shaking my head like I've just had an epiphany, and all this fuss over a two-month affair is just ridiculous. But I don't feel it. Not at all.

"Allie, I..."

"No, no," I say, holding up a hand to stop him. The coat and two bobble hats that I came to collect are still hanging in the hallway where I left them, so I grab them and shove them under my arm.

"Save it," I say. I can barely see straight, I'm so pissed.

I notice a few scarves that are mine and add them to the pile under my arm.

"I hope you have fun when you get back to the city. And have a nice life, *Mr. Blair!*"

I storm back out and slam the door behind me. I barely get two steps before I'm yanked back so hard I almost fall over.

No, it's not one of those cheesy romance movies where the guy stops the girl with a heart-churning kiss. I caught one of my scarves in the door.

The door clicks and Greyson pulls it open, looking up at me.

He looks so deeply, profoundly sad that I can barely stand to look at him. But I will not cry in front of him and I will not give in to the desire to comfort him.

"You caught your—" he starts.

"*Scarf!* I know," I huff, pulling it free and shoving it deeper into the pile under my arm. I flash him one last angry glance, before turning on my heels and storming off to my car. I throw the pile of clothes angrily onto the back seat, slam the car door shut, and peel away like I'm leaving the pitstop at the Indy 500.

It's not until I'm halfway along Old Green Road that the first tears sting my eyes, but by the time I get home I can barely see through the haze. And one look in the mirror is enough to know that I'm gonna need to stock up on cucumbers.

CHAPTER 22

Greyson

Two days after I arrive in LaGuardia, I'm sitting in my car, heading into the office to meet with Lincoln Peterson.

No, this isn't a second meeting. He sent me a text the day I came home, an hour before we were due to meet, canceling. This is what he considers a "power move." It accomplished nothing, except to reinforce that I did indeed miss Lottie's show and fuck things up with Allie for no reason whatsoever. And that I fucking hate Lincoln Fucking Peterson.

I don't have enough time to call into Ethan's office before I meet with Peterson, but I do stop by the bathroom and check myself in the mirror. Considering that I feel like dog shit, I don't actually look that bad. A little tired maybe, like I had a late night, but nowhere near as bad as I feel. I straighten my tie, sigh without looking myself in the eye, and head off to the boardroom.

The whole office is decked out for Christmas, which is barely two weeks away now, and the cheerful, celebratory mood feels grotesque to me.

Peterson is already in the boardroom, sitting next to his PA. He's taken the seat at the head of the huge, solid oak table, just like he always does. Ben's laptop is open on the table a few seats down and Ben himself is on his feet, pouring coffees.

"Oh, the wanderer returns," says Peterson as I enter, smirking in the most punchable way I've ever seen.

My lips twitch in response, but no smile appears on my face.

"What do you want, Lincoln?" I ask, sitting down.

It's not my usual style. I'm the one that gets sent into situations like this, when an awkward client is on the warpath, specifically because I'm good at schmoozing them. But not today.

The clinking of Ben's spoon against the side of his cup abruptly stops, and he comes over to sit beside me. I get the distinct impression that he thinks I need a minder.

I'm already furious at Lincoln. I fucked everything up with Allie and broke a promise to the sweetest little girl in the world, and then he had the temerity to cancel on me. Screw this guy.

"Well that's no way to talk to your biggest client," he says, bristling.

I stare at him silently, and out of the corner of my eye, I see his PA exchange a wary glance with Ben.

"Uh," says Ben, turning his laptop around to me. "Here's the account."

"I've seen it," I say, still staring directly at Peterson.

Maybe I'm not even angry at him. Maybe I'm angry at myself for giving in to the whims of this obnoxious asshole. Maybe I'm seething, churning on the inside because of my own, unforgivable assholery. Because I proved myself right. Because I hurt people. Again. Because I never told Allie exactly how I felt and that I would crawl over broken glass if it meant we could be together.

Because I'm a coward. A coward who runs away and hurts people.

"Well then, you know it's underperforming," says Peterson, with an indignant sniff.

I feel my jaw clench. I feel the joints on either side of it poke out under my cheeks. And I know Peterson sees it too because there's a flash of uncertainty across his detestable face.

I take in a long, deep breath through my nose, and breathe it out slowly. I'm usually an ocean of calm, but I am really struggling to keep my temper in check today. Taking Ben's laptop, I pull up some screenshots of the latest ad campaign for Peterson's company, and turn the screen around to face him.

"What do you see here, Lincoln?" I ask.

"My ad account," he says, frowning.

"No, no," I say, sharply. "What exactly do you see?"

Ben clears his throat beside me, but I ignore him.

"Get to the point, Blair," says Peterson, cocking up his nose. He's trying to look affronted but I can tell I have him on the back foot. And much to my surprise, I *like* the way it makes me feel. It gives my anger an outward target, and the brief respite from hating myself makes the rage almost cathartic.

"The point, Peterson," I say, all but spitting his last name. He flinches, and I press on, like a tiger stalking down my prey. "What you're looking at here is bad ad copy. And I don't just mean bad, I mean it's absolute dog shit."

His PA's eyes go wide as saucers, and Peterson sputters.

"Now listen here, I pay goo—"

"No, you listen!" I say, not realizing I've shouted it from my feet until Peterson stands up as well, a split second too slow to hide his shock. "You insisted on this ad copy. We told you. Cecie told you, Ethan told you, I told you. Fuck, I even tried to get Ben to tell your PA," I say. "This is what you pay us for. But no. You had to have this pile of unmitigated shit."

"Boss…" says Ben, quietly.

I ignore him, feeling myself swell with unspent wrath.

"And why? Because Lincoln Fucking Peterson is a narcissistic asshole who thinks he knows better than everyone else, that's why."

It feels good. I wish it didn't, but shouting in the face of this insufferable shit is the best I've felt since Sunrise Valley.

"Boss!" hisses Ben.

"Outrageous!" Peterson shouts. "I won't be talked to like this by… by some jumped up little prick who couldn't be bothered to answer calls. Be—" he hesitates. But he's started now, so he has to finish. "Because he was getting his dick wet with some whore in bumfuck nowhere!"

Ethan must have told him, while he was making excuses for me. A smug little smirk lifts onto Peterson's face. But only for a fraction of a second.

Because the fraction of a second after that, he's up against the boardroom wall, my knuckles white as they grip his expensively tailored lapels, and my face is barely an inch away from his.

"Say it again!" I snarl. A fleck of my spit lands on the end of his nose, but he's too petrified to even react. "Say it again, you vile little shit!"

Ben is trying to tear me off him with no success. I pull my fist back, savoring the thought of how it's going to feel to finally give this prick the beating he so richly deserves... and then something suddenly clamps tightly around my arm, and I'm being dragged backward, away from Peterson and out of the boardroom. Peterson slides down the wall, his jacket and tie askew and a look of sheer terror on his face.

"Greyson!" shouts Ethan, right beside my ear. I realize it's his hand on my arm. "Stop!"

I look at him, my eyes wild, and then back into the boardroom where Peterson is being helped to his feet by Ben and his PA. He's staring at me through the glass and, though I can't hear him, it's pretty clear that he's directing a stream of obscenities at me.

I'm not done. I want to lay into him with my fists and my feet and spend every ounce of my madness on him. I try to yank my arm free of Ethan's grip, to get back on the other side of that glass and finish what I started.

And then I feel an almighty crack on my jaw, and I stumble backward until I hit up against the wall.

With my hand on my face, I look at Ethan and realize he's socked me in the jaw. He's still standing there, arm cocked, looking ready to hit me again if I need it. But the shock has caused my anger to subside a little, and in any case, I'm distracted by the sudden throb that explodes across my head. I open my mouth wide and dig the heel of my palm into the spot where he punched me, trying to rub the pain away.

"Get back to work!" Ethan barks. I belatedly notice that a gaggle of employees have gathered to watch the scene, and are staring at me like I'm a madman. The tone of Ethan's command is so out of character that they scatter within seconds.

"You need to go home," he says, looking back at me with abject disappointment. "And let me try to fix this fucking mess."

"I…" I begin, but he cuts me off with a glare.

"LEAVE."

His tone makes it clear that this is not a discussion. Still holding my jaw, my head low as I try to avoid being seen, I stalk out of the office and leave Ethan to pick up the shattered remains of our company.

CHAPTER 23

Allie

My name is Alora Brooks and I am completely fine.

This is my mantra, and I've been playing it on repeat in my head ever since Greyson left, almost a week ago. Today, I even believed it enough to venture out of town to pick up the girls' Christmas gifts, while they stay with their aunt Sadie and make Christmas cookies.

Or maybe it was out of necessity. I've gotten hardly any of the Christmas prep done, having spent the last week moping, and the month before that frolicking about like a teenager with Greyson. And fixing up the mansion. And working in the diner.

So now I'm driving home in the dim light of the setting sun, with the girls' presents already wrapped and packed away in the trunk. I must still be pretty distracted, though, because I don't even realize I'm on Old Green Road until Sunrise

Valley House comes into view. My heart flips over in my chest at the surprise of seeing the old place, and then lands with a thud when I realize that the house has been painted a dull grey color. I can see a little sign as I get closer, and my heart rate picks up. When I'm close enough to see the big, red letters spelling out FOR SALE, I know I'm done for.

I barely get halfway to town before I have to pull over on the side of the lonely road. The tears have started again, and my vision is too obscured for me to drive safely. And my legs suddenly feel like jelly—I'm not sure I could brake in a hurry if I needed to.

All I can see is Greyson's smiling face as we argued about the best color to paint the mansion. And then my mind, treacherous as it is, is flooded with memories of all the good times. Kissing him in the puddle, snowball fights, Christmas fairs, and lazing in bed, limbs entangled.

And now he's gone, and the house is going to be sold.

He's never coming back.

My grip tightens on the steering wheel and I squeeze until my knuckles whiten. And then I scream. As loud as I can. I scream until my throat hurts and my face is red and my breath runs out.

And then the car door suddenly opens, and I nearly jump out of my skin. I look up, and through the haze of tears, I see Sam's concerned face looking down at me. He looks almost ready to cry himself. I must be a mess.

"Oh, Allie," he says, crouching down to reach in and hug me. He holds me tight and doesn't let go, and my entire body is wracked with sobs that have been unspent for a week because I've had to hold it together for the girls.

"Come on," he says when my sobs have subsided and I'm left with a blotchy face and some juddering sniffles. "We'll pick your car up later. Come with me."

I let him pull me out of the car and walk with him to his truck. As we climb in, he looks over at me and offers a gentle smile.

"We're gonna take care of you, sweetie. You'll see."

❄

"Allie's here!" he calls as we step through the door.

Drew pokes his head out from the kitchen, smiling.

"Great," he says. "I'll put on some extra pasta. Do you like carbonara, Allie?"

He takes one look at me and his smile drops. He disappears for a moment back into the kitchen, and when he reappears he's holding a bottle of wine and two glasses. I break into a chuckle for the first time in I don't know how long. It feels good.

"Don't let 'em get you down, sweetheart," winks Drew. "Dinner will be about twenty. And then you two can get sloshed and I'll be your babysitter."

"Thanks, Drew," I say, heading through into the living room with Sam.

Once I'm settled on the sofa, glass in hand, Sam disappears into the kitchen for a few minutes. He comes back to tell me that Sadie is keeping the kids tonight, Eddie has collected my car already, and that I'm staying here with him and Drew.

"No arguments, no protests, this is the judge's final decision!" he grins.

The meal is delicious, the wine flows freely, and the conversation is easy and light, the way it always is between old friends. It feels wonderful to let my hair down a little, to enjoy myself without having to keep up a front for the people who depend on me. And Sam and Drew both intuitively avoid mentioning Greyson for as long as I do.

Which is roughly until I'm halfway through my third glass of wine.

"You know," I say, my speech just a little slurred. "What an absolute shit."

"Absolutely!" says Sam, lifting his wine glass in a slightly drunken toast. Drew nods, sipping on the same beer he started during dinner.

"I mean, what a complete bastard," I say.

"Completely!" says Sam.

"Grey. Imagine painting it grey!" I snort.

"The house?" asks Drew.

"The house," says Sam.

"I miss him," I say, my face crumpling.

Sam seems to spring into action immediately, like he's been waiting for this moment all night. He scoots across the couch and puts his arm around me, giving my shoulders a squeeze.

"I let him so close to the girls," I sniff. "I was so stupid."

"No you weren't," says Sam. "You weren't. He seemed nice. You couldn't have known."

"I need to contact him," I say miserably. "I need him to send me an invoice to close the contract on HelpForHire. But I really don't want to do it."

"Email?" asks Sam.

I nod, sniffing again.

"Give me your phone," says Sam. "I'll do it."

I don't even hesitate, despite the fact that Sam is on his fourth glass of wine. The prospect of not having to spend an hour agonizing over every word I send him is too good to pass up. So I log into HelpForHire on my phone and hand it right over to Sam.

"So what did you get for the girls?" asks Drew, and I smile as I wipe my eyes, glad to change the subject back to happier things. I tell Drew all about Lottie and Emma's gifts, while Sam's thumbs patter furiously across my phone.

I don't even check what Sam's written when he hands my phone back, because Drew is regaling me with the story of how Jimmy Junior tried to impress some girl at the Christmas Fair by playing Pin the Tail on the Turkey with his legs tied together and fell flat on his ass.

CHAPTER 24

Greyson

BANG BANG BANG!

I peel one eye open at the sound of a loud hammering on my apartment door, and for a second I feel like I'm back in Sunrise Valley House, with the plumbers stomping around as they pull the upstairs bathroom apart. Christ, will I ever escape the sound of banging first thing in the morning?

I glance over at my blackout curtains. A narrow beam of light is infiltrating my room between them, bright enough to tell me it's daytime. Groaning, I reach over from the couch and slap my hand about until I find my phone on the coffee table. Shit, it's 1:24 pm.

Ignoring the three-digit bubble notifications on all my messaging and email apps, I drop the phone back onto the table and close my eyes again.

My head is throbbing. I've had this low-level stress headache since the day of the girls' concerts back in Sunrise Valley, but I haven't taken anything for it. Partly because it's a distraction from thinking about Allie. From remembering the smell of her hair and the sparkle of her eyes and wishing I was back there with her. And partly because I feel like I deserve the pain after all the shit I've caused for everyone.

There's another loud bang on the door. Rolling onto my side, I grab a cushion and hold it against the side of my head to drown out the noise. And then, I hear a muffled voice coming through the door.

"If you don't open it, I'm going to break it down!"

Ethan.

"Fucksake," I grumble, throwing the cushion across the darkened room. I get up from the couch—too fast, as it turns out—and almost keel over as the blood rushes to my head. It's little wonder; I sat on that couch all day yesterday and fell asleep on it in the early hours of the morning. This is the first time I've stood up in a while.

"Last chance!" I hear Ethan calling through the door.

"I'm coming!" I grumble. I take a moment to steady myself on my feet, then I walk over to the door and pull it open.

Ethan is standing there in his suit. He must have come from the office.

"What do you want?" I demand, irritably.

I haven't seen him since the Peterson incident, and the look on his face tells me that the "sabbatical" I've been taking hasn't done me any good.

"You look like shit," he says, pushing past me. He marches right across the room to the curtains and flings them open.

"Jesus Christ," I exclaim, squinting in the sudden brightness. I close the door and wait for my eyes to adjust, as Ethan takes in his surroundings.

Now that I look at it, it's a bit of a mess. There are half-empty takeout cartons and water bottles all over the place, dirty clothes on the floor, and the couch has a literal outline of my body pressed into it. Ethan turns around slowly, surveying the scene until he's finally facing me again. His face is a mixture of disgust and pity.

"What are you *doing?*" he says, exasperated.

"What do you mean?"

"*Look* at this place," he says, gesturing around. "And look at yourself."

I turn to the full-length mirror beside me and stare. My hair is holding the imprint of the cushion on one side, probably because I haven't showered in a few days, and there are big, dark bags under my eyes. The swelling has gone down on my jaw, at least, but he's not wrong. I look like shit.

"I'm depressed," I say to my reflection.

"You're not depressed," Ethan says. "Depressed people can't do anything about being depressed. You can fix everything wrong with your life with a single plane ticket."

I stare at him like he's crazy.

"What the fuck are you talking about?"

"Go back to Sunrise Valley, you dipshit," he says. He sounds almost angry that he has to spell it out for me like this.

A bitter laugh escapes my lips. "No."

"There's no reason for you to be in the city. You can work remotely for most of the stuff you do. And if you do need to attend a meeting in person, it's an hour's flight."

"No."

"You love her," he says.

"Doesn't matter." I say it almost defiantly.

Ethan sighs, then grimaces with disgust as he picks up a half-empty pizza box and carries it into the kitchen.

"Is this about Olivia?" he asks.

My gut flips over at the mention of her name, and I scowl at him. Anger comes to me so easily since I left Sunrise Valley.

"So what if it is?"

I've spent most of the last couple of weeks trying to keep Olivia out of my mind, ever since I got back from Sunrise Valley. Because every time I think of her, I see it—I see the pattern, more clearly than I ever have before. Olivia, her sunken cheeks and needle marks. Allie's anguished tears. I can imagine the disappointment on Lottie's face when she realized I had broken my promise, and it makes me want to curl up in a ball until the sun burns itself out.

Ethan is looking straight at me, impassive. His expression barely moves.

"It wasn't your fault."

We've never actually talked about this before. Not the gory details. He was always there for me, always knew what was going on—but he never pried, never judged, and certainly never said anything like this to me. Judging by how angry it's making me now, perhaps he was worried that I'd push him away if he said anything, and then I'd really have been lost.

"Then whose fault was it?" I ask, angrily.

"Hers," he replies, firmly. "Or nobody's. Sometimes, shit just happens."

"Well, shit wouldn't have happened if I'd done what you said and stayed here."

"Get over yourself."

He says it in such a deadpan, matter-of-fact way, like he's been waiting to say it for a decade, that it instantly infuriates me. I swing my head around to look at him.

"What did you say?"

"You heard me," he says. "Get over yourself. You think you're so special that the only thing it took for Olivia to fuck up her whole life was you leaving?"

I don't say anything, but I can feel the words seeping into me as my mind struggles to absorb them. It makes me uncomfortable, like there's something crawling under my skin.

"You tried to help her for two years, Greyson, and it nearly killed you. You have to let it go. Go back to Sunrise Valley and see Allie."

The sound of her name makes my heart ache.

"I don't deserve he—"

"So don't do it for you. You think Allie deserves to be unhappy?" he asks. "Because she seemed pretty happy to me, at Thanksgiving. With you."

Fuck. I glower at him, not willing to accept that he might be right.

"What happened with Peterson?" I ask, changing the subject like a churlish teenager. That seems to be my brand, these past few weeks.

Ethan sighs, shaking his head, but he indulges me.

"He's gone. Account closed."

"Shit," I say.

"Funny thing, though," says Ethan, poking an abandoned takeout carton with his boot. He's obviously given up on trying to tidy the place. I don't blame him.

"Turns out the fact that we had him on our books was putting other clients off working with us. Since word spread that he's gone, we're getting ten new client queries a week."

I stare at him, my brows raised in surprise.

"No shit?" I say. "What about legal?"

"He dropped it," Ethan says. "I told him that if he tried to sue us I'd release the security footage of him cowering on the boardroom floor like a little bitch."

I stare at him, hardly believing what I'm hearing.

"And he just dropped it?"

Ethan shrugs. "I mean he blustered a bit and called me a son of a bitch, but yeah. He's a narcissist. The last thing he wants is a video out there of him being a coward."

"So... it's all okay?" I ask.

"It's mostly okay," Ethan says, raising a brow at me. "You'll have to apologize to the staff members you traumatized in the hallway. But yes."

I can't believe it. Peterson is gone—for good—and the company is going to be just fine. I'm not sure if I'm relieved, or devastated that I left Allie for something that's been resolved so easily. If I'd known that all it would take to get rid of Peterson was threatening to beat him senseless, I'd have done it years ago.

"I've told everyone you're taking some time off and you'll be back in the new year," says Ethan, heading for the door. "You're welcome to come to us for Christmas, Greyson. But I hope you'll be somewhere else." He gives me a final nod as he pulls the door closed after him.

The thought of Christmas in Sunrise Valley, with Allie and the girls and the rest of her family… there's literally nothing on this Earth I'd love more. I look around my empty, fetid apartment, and the contrast couldn't be sharper. It really is a state. And I really do need to get a grip of myself. Ethan's words about Olivia keep churning in my mind as I start picking up boxes and bottles and the unidentifiable remnants of two-day-old take-out meals.

Have I really spent all these years blaming myself out of an overblown sense of my own importance? Or maybe, after two years of being slowly torn apart, was it just a way of convincing myself never to get involved with anyone else? Have I just been too scared—scared of going through something like that again—to take a chance?

I finish my first sweep of the apartment and stand back to admire it with an appropriately minor amount of satisfaction. I wouldn't call it *clean*, but it's at least fit for human habitation now. Recalling all those unread messages on my phone from earlier, I pick up my laptop and sit down on the couch. I may be taking some time off, but I can at least reply to all the people I've been ignoring.

I'm scrolling through my inbox when I notice an email from HelpForHire.

. . .

```
Hi, Gresyonblair! You have a new message
from Alora Brooks. Click here to read it.
```

My heart jumps into my throat, and I click the link before I've even finished reading the message. Sure enough, there in my HelpForHire inbox is a message from Allie. My hands are actually trembling as I open it and scroll down to read.

```
Hey, Asshole.
```

Not how I'd imagined Allie starting this mail—I was expecting something cold and formal—but fair enough. I did skip town on her and break a promise to her daughter. Despite the rocky opening, I'm still tingling with excitement to hear from her.

```
It's Sam.
```

Oh.

```
First of all, I want you to know that I
think you're a real douche for skipping
town.
```

Can't argue with that.

. . .

```
And second of all, Allie needs you to wind
down the account on here so she can do
something with payments.
```

My heart sinks. This account is my very last connection to Allie. And it's the way we met. Winding it down feels like it would be the end of this chapter of my life, and as I think about it I realize I'm not so sure I'm ready to do that.

```
And last, because she'd never tell you
herself: she really misses you. She had big
feelings for you and you just took them and
stomped them under your boot, like an
asshole (see above). And you should know
that, because I see no reason you should be
breezing around the big apple while my
friend sits here trying to hide her puffy
eyes from her little girls.
```

Every word of it hits me like a slug in the gut. Not the parts about me being an asshole, I can't argue with that (see above). But the bits about Allie being sad, and crying, and trying to hide it from the girls. I can't stand it.

```
Anyway. Do the account thing. Please.
```

```
Sam.
```

. . .

> Sometimes you never know the value of a moment until it becomes a memory.

My breath hitches as I read the bright purple text of the last line. I stare at it for a long moment, and suddenly I'm transported back to my first day in Sunrise Valley House, when I first saw that line in its stupid Comic Sans font. God, why did it annoy me so much back then? It seems such a silly thing to be irritated by.

And then, as though triggered by the recollection of how it all began, memories of Allie begin to flood through my mind. The first day she came to the house. Her Care Bears hat. Meeting the girls in the diner when they were on the hunt for cookies. Singing Bon Jovi as we barreled down the highway. Fixing the tap with her. Our kiss in the mud. Our night together in the snowed-in mansion. Thanksgiving. Playing Santa at the Christmas fair. Decorating the tree.

The antlers and that *terrible* French accent.

Tears are streaming down my face, happy tears shaken loose by the sheer joy of the memories flowing through me, and I can't help it anymore. I throw back my head and start laughing uncontrollably.

"HOLY SHIT!" I say out loud, to nobody. "IT'S TRUE!" The stupid purple Comic Sans email signature is *true!*

I'm still laughing like a maniac as I reach for my phone and hit the speed dial. It barely rings once before a voice on the other end answers.

"Boss?"

"MERRY CHRISTMAS, BEN!" I practically shout down the line.

There's a long pause, and then Ben speaks again, carefully, as though not wanting to upset the madman on the other end.

"Boss, it's December 18th."

"I know, Ben. I know! But do you know what that means?"

"What does that mean?" he says, his voice warming a little, with a hint of a smile in it.

"It means I've got a week! But there's a *shit ton* I need to do, and there's no way I can do it without you. Will you help me? Please?"

Another pause, shorter this time, and then Ben answers. His voice still sounds a little bemused, but I can practically hear his grin from here.

"What do you need, G?"

"Give me ten minutes and I'll send over a list."

My mind is already racing, planning, going over everything that I'll have to put in place.

"No problem. Send over whatever you have and I'll get started on it."

"Thanks, Ben. Thanks a million. I'll talk to you soon."

"Talk soon. And G?"

"Yes, Ben?"

"It's good to have you back."

CHAPTER 25

Allie

"Hey!" I call as I push open the door of Sadie's house, knocking twice as a courtesy before I let myself in. It's the day before Christmas Eve, and the girls and I have come over for a visit. They both push past me, giggling gleefully, and run off to find their cousins.

"Hey!" calls Sadie from the kitchen. "Come on in."

I peek into the sitting room on my way, just in time to see the girls giving Eddie a big hug, and we exchange nods as I pass by and head down the hall to the kitchen.

Sam and Drew are sitting at the table, and they both look up at me as I enter. They seem a little... nervous, I guess?

"Oh, hey, you two!" I say. I wasn't expecting to see them here.

"Sit down," says Sadie, waving me to a seat.

"O...kay," I say, looking from her to Drew and across to Sam. "What's going on?"

Sam clears his throat. "We've… got something to tell you," he says, with some difficulty.

I look around at the three of them again, and this time I notice the concern etched on their faces. My stomach begins to churn a bit. What's going on?

"Allie," says Sadie, sitting down next to me. She holds my hand, gently, and it feels so much like the day she told me Libby had died that a nervous tension spikes immediately in my gut.

"What is it?" I demand, my voice higher than I intended.

"Listen. We didn't want you to find out from anyone else, but Sam was driving on Old Green Road earlier, and… well…"

I look at Sam, who's looking right back at me with wide, sad eyes.

"The sign's gone," he says.

It takes me a moment to realize what he's talking about.

"And there were moving trucks in the drive."

A cold tingle travels all the way up my legs and down my arms. The mansion has sold. Greyson's last tie to Sunrise Valley is severed.

He's not coming back.

"Are you all right?" Sadie asks when I don't say anything.

No. I am definitely not all right. The sadness that had settled in behind my sternum is roaring back to life, and I can feel a lump rising in my throat.

"Ye—" I start. I cut off when my voice cracks and clear my throat. "Yeah," I say. "I'm fine."

"You know, it's all right not to be fine, Allie," says Drew. "It's a big deal."

Tears sting my eyes and I try to blink them back. I know I've failed when Sam plucks a tissue out of the box on the table and hands it to me.

"Stay here tonight," says Sadie. "Even if you spend the night in the spare room by yourself. At least I'll be here to look after the girls."

I dab at my tear-wetted cheeks and nod, grateful for the offer. I'm so tired of constantly having to hold it together on the outside while I fall apart inside.

"And tomorrow as well," she says. "The girls' gifts are in our garage anyway. We'll just leave a sign outside. You know… for Santa."

I've scraped together enough gifts to make sure the girls will have a good Christmas, but I know they can both tell I'm not feeling a hundred percent. They've both been unusually well behaved the past couple of weeks, and they keep giving me random cuddles and saying "Poor Mommy."

It breaks my heart every time.

If I stay here tomorrow night, they'll at least have the excitement of their cousins to keep them entertained. And I'll have Sadie and Eddie to keep me going if I falter.

I nod gratefully, giving Sadie a watery smile.

"Thank you."

"Any time," she says. "You know that. We can wrap gifts later and chat about what a shithead Douchebag McFuckface is."

We all laugh together, and I wipe yet more tears from my face.

After dinner, when Sam and Drew have departed with promises to see us all on Christmas Day, and Sadie has insisted on looking after the girls for the evening, I head upstairs and slide into a long-overdue bubble bath. I wish I could say that it melted all my troubles away, that I relaxed and gained some perspective and realized that I was better off without Greyson. But the truth is that I just sat there, adding my tears to the water until it turned cold, feeling like a part of me was missing and that I'd never get it back.

❄

It's Christmas Eve, and the kids have been bouncing around with anticipation all day. We'd hoped that they'd run out of energy at some point, but as time wears on it's becoming clear that's not going to happen. In an effort to tire them out so they'll be able to sleep, we take a long walk up the same hill we hiked on Thanksgiving afternoon.

I'm holding out okay until we reach the summit, and I remember being up here with Greyson. I miss the feeling of his arms around me as we stood and watched Sam declare his undying love for Drew. I miss the taste of his lips and the smell of his hair. And I miss the way he looked at me like there was nobody else in the world he'd rather look at.

It makes it even harder to accept that he just… left.

"Mommy! Help!" shouts Lottie, giggling as she runs right into my leg.

"Oof!" I say, just as River comes running over and touches Lottie on the arm.

"Tag!" she shouts, and they both run away in peals of laughter.

"How are you holding up?" asks Sadie, coming over to stand beside me. She loops her arm through mine as we start back down the hill.

"Oh, you know," I say, shrugging. "I'm all right."

We get back to the house just in time for supper, and afterward, we put out the sign we spent the afternoon making on the front lawn, to let Santa know that Lottie and Emma Brooks are staying in this house tonight. Just to be on the safe side, you understand. We hang the stockings over the fireplace, scatter some cookies on a plate, and set them out with a glass of milk for Santa and a carrot for Rudolph.

Lottie insists on getting more carrots for the other reindeer because it's not fair that only Rudolph gets one. Once the kids are satisfied that everything is just right for Santa's visit, we take them up to bed, read them their stories, and restate the importance of going to sleep early so Santa can stop by.

Sadie, Eddie, and I sit around the twinkling Christmas tree, drinking tea and chatting in hushed tones until we're sure the kids are asleep. And then the traditional Christmas Eve frenzy begins. Eddie brings in all the gifts from their hiding-place in the garage, and Sadie and I set them out in little piles for each of the kids.

We unbox the gifts that need to be assembled, shushing each other when the rip of a box opening is too loud. Eddie has his toolbox beside him and murmurs obscenities to himself as he tries to find the right sized Philips-head screwdriver to put together a bike for Finn, and then a somewhat more distinct stream of obscenities when he realizes that he's forgotten to attach the stabilizers and has to start over.

Sadie and I, meanwhile, are a whirlwind of scissors and wrapping paper and tape as we wrap the gifts and put them under the tree. We spend a good ten minutes arguing over whether the bike needs to be wrapped. At several points, we swear that we're not going to leave this until Christmas Eve next year, just like we did last year and the year before that.

When we're all done, Sadie hands me a glass of red wine.

"We deserve it," she winks, and the three of us clink our glasses together to toast another successful year of pulling the wool over our children's eyes.

"We do," I agree, taking a sip and looking over the plateau of gifts laid out before us.

I still have that hollow feeling inside. I always knew that Greyson would be leaving, but I somehow also imagined spending this evening with him, curled up on the sofa with the girls in bed, and the Christmas tree twinkling beside the roaring fire.

I can at least be excited on the girls' behalf, and tomorrow I'll be surrounded by family. Even my mom and dad are making the journey up to see us. It's more than a lot of people have to look forward to, and I try to focus on that instead of dwelling on the things I don't have.

"We do," I say again. "I can't wait to see their faces in the morning."

CHAPTER 26

Allie

"He caaaame!" screams Lottie, launching herself onto my bed with Christmas stocking in hand.

It takes me a moment and four deep blinks to realize where I am, what day it is, and what she's talking about. Remind me never to drink on Christmas Eve again. It was only a couple of glasses, but I can feel it in the dryness of my mouth and the fuzziness of my head as I push myself up to sit on the bed beside Lottie.

"Look!" calls Emma.

Outside the bedroom door, I can see her dragging her stocking along behind her. Laughing, I grab my phone to snap a quick picture before helping Emma to get herself and her stocking up onto the bed.

There are whoops and squeals as they pull out the trinkets and treats I've stuffed in their stockings. I think their excitement is infectious because I actually feel relatively content this morning. More than I was expecting, at any rate.

Lottie looks up at me, beaming with delight, and bobs her head from side to side to show me how the stars on her new hairband bounce around.

"Wow!" I grin. "That's so cool!"

Once their stockings are emptied, we all head to the bathroom to clean up and get dressed. Last year I made the mistake of letting them get downstairs and open their gifts first. Never again. They were still in pajamas and playing with their new toys five minutes before we had to leave for dinner.

In an effort to make myself feel better, I'm wearing a Santa hat, a chunky cream sweater, and a mid-thigh tartan red skirt over woolly black tights and knee-high boots. I let the girls choose their own outfits today, so Emma is wearing a purple and blue tutu over leggings with a t-shirt that has a pug's face on it. Lottie has opted for thick tights with a dinosaur-print dress my mom made for her last year.

There's a flurry of activity in the hall as Sadie, Eddie, and the kids appear from their room. The kids are all bright-eyes and sunbeams, desperate to get downstairs and see what Santa's left for them. Sadie, Eddie, and I trudge along behind them, bleary-eyed but smiling at the chaos unfolding around us.

"Look, Mommy!" shouts Lottie. Every time she opens something, she is absolutely overwhelmed with joy.

I didn't manage to get them everything I wanted to, and River and Finn have a few more gifts than my girls, but the unbridled happiness that comes pouring out of them every time they open a new gift brings tears to my eyes. They really are great kids.

When they've opened all their gifts, and the adults are no longer required to sit and look surprised and amazed with each new reveal, Sadie heads into the kitchen to brew some coffee while Eddie and I collect the discarded bows, boxes, and wrapping paper.

"It's magical, huh?" asks Eddie, nodding toward the kids.

I look over at them, all happily playing with their new toys. River and Lottie are laughing and chasing River's new robot dog around the room, Emma is putting a plastic ice-cream together with her new kitchen playset, and Finn is laying on his stomach, his tongue poking out as he concentrates with all his might on clicking his Legos together.

"Ah, to be a kid again," I smile.

"You okay?" he asks, looking at me with a note of concern.

Christmas isn't easy for any of us since Libby's accident, and everyone knows that this year will be particularly tough for me.

"Yeah," I say, tying up the bag in my hands. I swallow down the lump in my throat and smile over at him. "I have a big brother who cares enough to ask me if I'm okay," I wink.

"Daaaad…" calls River.

We both turn around to see her standing at the window, looking out over the twinkling front lawn.

"What's that?" she jabs a finger at the window.

"What?" asks Eddie, tying the last of the wrapping paper up in a garbage bag.

"That big sack," says River.

The other kids have joined her at the window. I glance over at Eddie, he shrugs back at me, and we both head over to the window to see what's going on.

Out in the yard, just inside the gate, there's a giant, red velvet sack. The top is tied with a gold ribbon, and there's a card hanging off the bow.

I glance up at Eddie, and he looks down at me and shrugs again.

"Mom and Dad, maybe?" he says, but we're both a little skeptical. This isn't really their style. And they'll be here later for dinner anyway—why send a sack of presents ahead?

"I want to see!" says River, running out to the hall and grabbing up her hat and coat. We all follow suit, kids and adults alike, Eddie running into the kitchen to alert Sadie of the mystery sack that has appeared on their front lawn. Once we've all pulled on our boots and coats and flung our scarves around our necks, we tromp out onto the snowy front lawn.

River, as the first one to spot the sack, demands that she be the one to read the card. She reaches up, grabs the card, pulls it down in front of her face, and peers at it.

"It's for Lottie and Emma!" she calls.

Lottie gasps.

Sure enough, it does say "For Lottie and Emma," on the card. There's nothing else, and no "From."

"Mommy, can we look inside?" asks Lottie, her eyes huge as she looks up at me.

"Just a sec," I say, apprehensively. I'm not one to worry and believe all sorts of strange horror stories, but I don't know where the sack has come from, and I'm not about to let them dig into it without checking what's inside. I undo the beautiful golden bow that's wrapped around the top, and then—with a little more nervousness than I outwardly show—I pull it open.

Presents. There are presents inside. All different shapes and sizes, and wrapped with all different kinds of wrapping paper and glitter and bows.

I pull one out and shake it. It sounds innocuous enough. The card says "Lottie," so I crouch down beside her and stay very close while she opens it, using my hand to coax her into holding it at a slight distance.

"Oh my goodness!" she cries when she realizes what it is. It's the same robot dog she's been chasing around with River all morning. I almost gasp myself. This particular robot dog is this year's big thing, and by the time I was done moping over Greyson they were out of stock everywhere I looked.

I stay close for a few more gifts, a couple for Lottie and a couple for Emma, and once I'm satisfied that there's nothing sinister about the sack and its contents I let them carry on and go to stand with Sadie and Eddie.

"Did you do this?" I whisper.

They both look at me, shaking their heads.

"Hot dog!" cries Emma with delight. "Mommy it's from Santa!"

I look down at her and she's holding a painted wooden hot dog in her hands. My mind is ripped right back to the Christmas grotto, to the image of Emma sitting on Greyson's knee, happily swinging her legs and asking Santa to deliver her a hot dog on Christmas Day, and my throat is suddenly tight.

"Look! This one's for you, Mommy!" calls Lottie.

She's holding a little box in her hand, about the size of a deck of playing cards, and she brings it over to me.

"What the…" I lift up the card with slightly shaky hands and see only one word printed on it: "Allie."

I glance at Eddie and Sadie with a confused frown and they both nod for me to open the gift. I unwrap it carefully, pulling out a velvet-covered box from inside, and pop it open.

Sadie gasps beside me. "Is that…"

"Mommy, Mommy, let me see!" says Lottie, jumping up and down to try and look inside the box.

I'm frozen to the spot, completely speechless, and my mind is reeling.

Laying there on a silk cushion inside the box, held in place with a matching silk bow, is the key to Sunrise Valley House.

I'd recognize the intricate metalwork anywhere, but instead of the ancient, half-rusted key I had before, it looks brand new. It's either a copy or it's been cleaned up. And now it's here, in my hands.

"What's the card say?" asks Eddie.

It's only then that I notice the little tag that's attached to the key. I lift it up and there are tiny gold letters embossed into the thick paper:

USE ME

I have no idea what's happening. My feet begin to tingle, my head is light… I feel like Alice, tumbling down the rabbit hole into Wonderland. What does it mean? Does it mean Greyson is... *giving* me the house?

No.

He sold it.

Unless he didn't?

But then why were there moving trucks outside? And it's too big for me and the girls—I can't afford to run a house that size. And can I really accept this after what happened between us? What should I do?

"Allie?" asks Sadie. Her voice is distant and muffled as it pushes through the chatter in my head. It sounds like it's not the first time she's tried to get my attention.

I turn my head towards her and stare. The world feels unreal, like everything is a million miles away.

"We can watch the kids a while," she says.

Her meaning is as plain as day. I look down at the little box sitting on my upturned palm again.

I'm elated.

And sad.

And overjoyed.

And furious.

The emotions all churn inside me at once. I'm more confused than ever, but I have to go. I have to see.

I have to have some closure.

"Yeah," I say to Sadie, nodding. "Thanks."

❄

I'm not sure how I managed to get to Sunrise Valley House in my dreamlike state. But here I am, turning into the driveway in my clapped out little car with my heart beating so fast it's practically a hum.

I stop halfway along the drive when the house comes into view. There's something different about the place, and given the absolutely flummoxed emotional state I'm in, it takes me way longer than it should to realize what it is. As my addled mind catches up with my eyes, I give a little yelp of surprise.

It's yellow. The main body of the house has been painted yellow. THE yellow. The one I kept telling Greyson to use. It looks just as beautiful as I hoped it would.

That's not all. There are Christmas lights twinkling along the top of the porch, and I can see lights inside as well, and the shadow of a big Christmas tree just inside the window.

My bemused frown grows deeper. I can't see any other cars anywhere. Is this all for me? I pick up the little box and get out of my car, slamming the door behind me as I walk toward the house.

When I slide the glittering new key into the lock and turn it, the familiar clanking sound stops me short. The last time I heard it was the last time I saw Greyson, and I have to pause for a moment to swallow down the lump in my throat, before stepping into the house.

"Oh, my God," I gasp.

The hallway looks completely different, and it's spectacular. There's a big, thick rug on the floor and new furniture around the edges. The side table has an old-style phone sitting on it, and there's a little Christmas tree full of twinkling fiber-optic lights beside it. The feel of the place is modern, but it pays homage to the grand old Queen Anne architecture.

I've been holding my breath, I realize, when I start feeling light-headed again. But when I do inhale, my nostrils are filled with the scent of coffee and baking. And there's music floating into the hall from the kitchen, the door of which is open just a crack.

I close the space between myself and the door with two long strides and reach for the handle. The music is more distinct now, and very familiar:

"If you like Pina Coladas,

And getting caught in the rain…"

The dulcet tones of Rupert Holmes' voice are drowned out by the sound of blood rushing past my ears as my heart starts thundering in my chest again. I push the door open a crack more. The kitchen is totally different; the cabinets have been replaced, the stovetop is new, and all the counters are now a beautiful black marble. And there, standing beside the oven with his back to me, is Greyson.

He's moving steaming croissants from a baking tray onto a plate, swaying his hips to the upbeat music playing behind him. And he looks… *ridiculous*. He's wearing a bright red and green knit Christmas sweater with an elf on the back, and a pair of reindeer antlers just like the ones I was wearing the day we met.

The chorus of the song kicks in, and he starts singing along:

. . .

"If you like being a banana… and getting caught in the rain…"

I can't help myself. He looks so ridiculous, and the sound of him singing Emma's lyrics is just too much. I snort a laugh, and he immediately snaps his head around and looks right at me.

I'm rumbled.

To his credit, he doesn't smile at me, or act like everything is fine and he can simply pick up where we left off. Instead, he reaches over and clicks off the speaker, turns to face me, and takes a deep breath.

"Sorry," he says. "I thought it'd take longer for anyone to notice the sack."

I want to run to him and jump into his arms. And I want to scream at him and stomp my feet. I don't trust myself to say anything yet, so I just stare at him, my smile gone, waiting.

"Allie, I—"

As soon as he starts, I find my voice.

"Why are you here?" I ask, finally stepping into the kitchen. My voice is harsher than I want to be. Probably not as harsh as he deserves.

I fold my arms over my chest.

I still don't understand what's going on. I don't know why he's here, why the house is yellow, or why the inside is suddenly so warm and homey.

He frowns, looks down at his feet, and swallows.

"Allie," he says, stepping around the counter and moving a few paces toward me.

My heart does a victory dance in my chest, and my brain tells it to pipe the fuck down.

"Please, just… listen," he says.

I keep my arms folded and jut out my chin, giving him a nod to speak.

"God, you're sexy when you're pissed," he says, a hint of a smile on his face.

"Don't push your luck, Greyson," I warn him. "Say what you have to say."

His smile drops and he nods, reaching up to scratch nervously at the back of his head.

"Did you see the house?" he asks. "Before?"

"Of course I saw the house before, I helped you t—"

"No," he cuts in. "Not back then. I mean before yesterday."

I realize what he's asking. "It was grey," I reply, warily.

"Everything was grey," he says, taking another step. He's within arm's reach now. "Allie, everything's been grey in my life for a very long time. But I didn't know it. I didn't realize I was living this half-lived life, afraid of getting close to anyone in case I hurt them, and I—"

He cuts off when I snort derisively.

"I know," he says, his face imploring. "I know I did a shitty thing, and I will never, ever stop being sorry for it. Not ever. But I need you to know that you ruined me. You ruined everything about the life I had before I met you. Because when I was with you, I lived in glorious technicolor for the first time in as long as I can remember. And I loved it. I loved it. I loved... I love. I love, love, love you. I love you, Alora Brooks."

I'm still standing with my arms folded and my chin out, but I can feel tears springing to my eyes and my bottom lip quivering.

"Let me love you," he says. "Please."

"I let you close to the girls," I say, and the first tear finally falls down my cheek. "And you hurt them."

"Never again," he says quickly. The look on his face is dead serious. "Never, ever again. I want to be there for every school play, every birthday, every holiday. I want…"

He trails off and steps closer, running his finger along my cheek to wipe away the tear.

"Come with me," he says, holding out his hand. "Let me show you something."

I hesitate.

"Please."

I can feel my resolve weakening with every word he speaks. I hold out my hand and he pulls me back into the hall and up the stairs. The whole house is beautiful, but when he leads me to the door at the end of the hallway and pushes it open, I'm struck dumb.

There are two beds in the middle of the room, each carved in the shape of a different dinosaur, and draped with pale blue netting. There are toy shelves and bookshelves along each wall, wardrobes painted with chalkboard paint, and a desk in the corner with twinkle lights strung all over it. It's a child's bedroom. A magnificent, wondrous child's bedroom.

I look across at Greyson and he's staring at me intently, as though he's feasting on my reaction.

"You did this?" I ask.

"Mostly," he says. "I had some help from a designer friend who owed me a favor. Come on."

He grabs my hand again, pulls me back into the landing, and pushes open another nearby door.

"My office," he says. "I work here now. Permanently."

I don't have time to do anything but stare up at him, open-mouthed, before he leads me back down the stairs. He takes me all the way through the house to the back door and outside.

We traipse in silence through the patchy snow until we reach the outbuilding, right beside the tap where we had our first kiss. Greyson reaches into his pocket and pulls out a ring of keys. He flips through them until he finds the right one, then opens the padlock on the door and pulls it off.

"Look," he says, standing back, nodding to the door.

I give him a questioning glance and push the door open all the way. Greyson reaches inside and pulls a cord attached to the ceiling, and the whole place lights up.

"What the…" I say, taking a few steps inside.

The inside of the building has been insulated and paneled, and it actually manages to look bigger on the inside than it does from the outside. There's a desk in the corner with a laptop and what looks like a large flatscreen beside it; I recognize it as the most highly-regarded (and expensive) drawing tablet on the market. Behind the desk, there's a tall easel, and beside it a storage unit.

"Your studio," he says behind me.

A ripple runs up my back as I take it all in.

"Ben will work on your website with you."

I turn around. My face must be a picture of shock.

"It's yours whether you take me back or not," he says. "But God, I hope you do. I want to be with you. Forever. I want to stand guard over your dreams while you stand guard over the girls' dreams. And besides, I'm not sure I'd get much use out of a pair of custom-made dinosaur beds."

I laugh, and it's like a floodgate opening. The pent-up pressure of all the conflicting emotions I've been feeling comes out in a strange mixture of laughing and crying, and when Greyson steps closer, I reach up and grab around his neck. His arms wrap around me and pull me into him, holding me tight while I laugh-cry.

"Thanks for ruining my Christmas day makeup," I say, wiping my hand across my cheek.

"Allie," he says, seriously. "You haven't answered me."

"You haven't asked me," I sniff.

He pulls back to look down at me and pushes a curl out of my blotchy face. His eyes sparkle the same way they always do whenever my stubborn side comes out, and he shakes his head and sighs with mock exasperation.

"Fair enough," he says. "Alora Brooks.... no, wait."

He grabs my hand and pulls me outside, to the tap where we first kissed. The ground is covered in muddy slush where the snow has started melting, but he gets down on one knee regardless, and I think I might faint when he grabs my hand.

"Allie," he says. "I love you. I love the way you laugh and the way you frown. I love the way your little nose wrinkles in the middle when you don't like something but you're holding it in. I love the way you're so generous with everyone and so kind. But most of all, I love the way you speak French."

Tears are streaming down my face, but I burst out laughing.

"And I want to be with you every day, and live in this grand old mansion with you and the girls. Will you marry me?"

My face crumples and I nod, unable to say anything. He smiles the most radiant smile I've ever seen, rises to his feet, and kisses me in glorious technicolor.

CHAPTER 27

Greyson

I can't believe I'm standing here, in the very spot where I first kissed Allie, kissing her again. I can't believe she's agreed to marry me. In all of my wildest dreams of this moment, I never allowed myself to actually believe that it could all work out. And yet, I am. Here *we* are. If there's a happier man on the face of the planet, I can't imagine how.

The amount of favors I had to pull in to get the mansion ready by today has basically indebted me for life. But it was worth it, every bit, for the look on Allie's face as I showed her around her new home.

I spend a good fifteen minutes kissing her, like I'm afraid she'll disappear if I stop. Ten of those were after she got a call from Sadie to check that everything is all right. Five of them were after Allie told me we really needed to head back to Sadie's *right now* or we were going to miss Christmas dinner.

Between kissing my fiance (!!!) and rushing to get back in time, I didn't even think to change my pants. So I still have one muddy knee when we pull up outside Sadie and Eddie's place.

"I guess everyone hates me, huh?" I ask, grimacing towards the house.

"Definitely," she says, grinning at me as I sit folded up in the tiny space on the passenger's side. We *really* need to get her a new car.

"Actually, they probably just pretended to for my benefit. I'm sure they'll get over it when they see that I have." She pauses. "Well, fairly sure." She cocks her head like she's considering the question more deeply. "Well..." She gives me a thumbs-up with a supportive—but decidedly uncertain—look on her face. "I guess we'll find out soon!"

I struggle out across the driver's seat and clamber to my feet. Allie is waiting for me, and she reaches up to kiss my lips before we head inside.

"Moral support?" I ask.

She just laughs and pushes the door open.

"Oh, hey Greyson," says Eddie, without skipping a beat. Sadie probably warned him that I'd be coming after she called Allie back at the mansion. He's standing in the hallway, chewing, with a half-eaten canape in his hand. He lifts it up and extends a finger towards my pants.

"You've got mud on your knee," he says.

"Yeah," I nod. "I know. Hey, Merry Christmas."

He looks to Allie, and I guess she's smiling because he does, too. "Merry Christmas," he says, tossing the rest of the canape into his mouth.

"He... asked me to marry him," says Allie, glancing downwards bashfully.

Eddie's eyes go wide, and he looks from Allie to me and back again.

"And I said yes," she adds quickly.

Eddie swallows his canape, wipes his hand on his pants, and comes over to wrap us both into a bear hug.

"I knew you'd do the right thing, buddy!" he says. "Never doubted you for a second! I told Sadie—"

"Told Sadie what?" asks Sadie, appearing in the door with a dishtowel over her shoulder. She stops dead when she spots me, her face somehow both expressionless and disgusted at the same time.

"Oh, well if it isn't Runaway McCowardpants," she says.

"Er—honey," Eddie says, cutting in before Sadie has a chance to tell me what she *really* thinks. "They're getting married!"

Sadie's brows lift in surprise. She looks over at Allie, who nods back with a little smile.

"Oh!" Her face breaks into a grin as she comes over to give me a hug, pulling Allie in too. This is... quite an emotional rollercoaster. I'm half scared she's only hugging me so she can plunge a knife into my back.

"That's amazing!" Sadie says. "Well done you t—"

"Greyson!"

Lottie's voice drowns out everyone else as she comes rushing out of the living room towards me, arms wide open, and I scoop her up and hug her close. She squeezes so tight that I'm not sure whether she's trying to hug me or choke me out.

"Yuck!"

Emma has arrived to see what all the fuss is about, and now she's standing a few feet away, pointing at my muddy pants.

"Oh, you've got mud on your pants," says Sadie.

"He knows," Allie tells her.

"Hey, Emma," I say, crouching down with Lottie. I hold out my arm and Emma toddles over. As I squeeze them both, Lottie whispers quietly in my ear.

"We missed you."

I feel a lump rising in my throat, and a huge swell of contentment sweeps over me. It took me a while, but now I know that I'm exactly where I'm supposed to be.

Suddenly, there's a commotion behind us. Someone is trying to push through the front door, and it hits Sadie square in the back.

"Hey!" Sadie shouts, turning around towards the door.

"It's only us!" calls Sam.

Sadie shuffles away from the door to let them in, and Sam pecks a kiss on his sister's cheek as he enters. Drew walks in behind him, and then they both stop in their tracks.

Sam's eyes flick over to Allie. When he sees that she's smiling his concern fades, only to be replaced with his trademark sass.

"I knew you'd come crawling back," he says. "Never doubted it for a second."

Eddie, who seems to have an endless supply of canapes somewhere, addresses Sam through a mouthful of food. "They're getting married."

Sam pauses for a moment, dumbfounded, while the information slowly sinks into his brain. He glances over to Allie, who nods a confirmation back at him. And then a wide smile breaks out across his face, and he's back to his usual animated self.

"*Ahhhhh!*" squeals Sam, waving his hands around in front of him in excitement. He bypasses me completely to grab Allie into a massive hug.

"Bro," says Drew, nodding at my legs. "You've got mud on your p—"

"*He knows!*" says Allie, Eddie, and Sadie, all at the same time, and everyone laughs.

❄

Allie's parents arrive just after noon, and there's a big fuss because nobody has seen them in a while. When Allie introduces me and tells them we're getting married, her mother, Mary, cries tears of joy at the news that her youngest baby is going to be a bride. Derek, Allie's father, gives me a bone-crushing handshake and dryly tells me that he hopes I know what I'm in for.

Dinner is beautiful. Everyone gasps as Sadie sets down a huge glazed ham. Eddie carves it up and shares it out. Sam and Allie help Sadie to bring out dish after fancy dish of vegetables and other sides. By the time the meal is done, and all that's left on the table are dessert plates with the crumbs of a delicious pumpkin pie on them, we're all stuffed.

I hang back in the kitchen with Drew and Eddie to help with the cleanup, and then we all convene in the living room. I gratefully accept a beer from Eddie and, since there are no seats left, I lean against the wall near the door, watching Allie and Sam face off against Sadie and Drew in a highly competitive game of Pictionary.

"Greyson, do you have a minute?" asks Allie's mom, coming over to stand beside me.

"Sure, Mary," I smile, straightening. "What's up?"

She beckons me into the hallway and closes the door behind us.

"I'm so glad to see Allie happy," she says, and the crows' feet at the corners of her eyes crinkle when she smiles.

"Me too," I say.

I'm glad to see Allie happy. I'm glad to be able to make Allie happy. I've realized that my happiness is intrinsically linked to Allie's in a way that feels almost cosmic.

Mary takes my hand and pulls it toward her, then drops something small and warm into my palm.

"Here," she says. "Take this."

I look down at my palm and my brows shoot up in surprise.

"Yours?" I ask, looking back at Mary.

I see tears sparkling along her lower lids and she shakes her head.

"No, son. Not mine."

CHAPTER 28

Allie

After Sam and I have finished trouncing Sadie and Drew at Pictionary and I have performed the obligatory victory dance, I head off to find Greyson. I want to leave relatively early so we can get the girls back to the mansion, before they're too tired to appreciate their bedrooms or to understand what's happening.

I find him in the hallway with my mom, hugging her.

"Hey!" I say.

My mom breaks the hug and Greyson darts his hand into his pocket. As I get a little closer, I notice that my mom has been crying.

"Mom!" I place my hand on her arm and look her over with concern. "Are you all right?"

"Oh," she laughs, wiping her cheeks. "Yes, sweetheart. Just happy for you is all. You know how I am."

I smile and hug her. I can't blame her—this is a lot for your daughter to spring on you when you thought you were just coming over for a quiet Christmas dinner.

"I think we're going to head home," I say. "But I'll see you tomorrow so we can make sandwiches out of leftovers, right?"

"It's tradition!" she grins, kissing me on the cheek.

She pats Greyson's arm on the way past and goes back into the living room.

"What was that all about?" I ask, turning to Greyson.

He shrugs and pulls his hand out of his pocket, then wraps his arm around me and pecks an affectionate kiss on the top of my head.

"Shall we go home, then?" he asks.

It's so strange to know that by "home" he means the mansion. That beautiful old house is where I live, now. With Greyson and the girls. A smile spreads across my face and I nod.

"Yes. Let's go home."

❄

The girls were ecstatic when they saw their room. Lottie teared up, and Emma spent no less than twenty full minutes jumping up and down on her new bed. It took a good hour and a cup of cocoa each to calm them down enough to sleep, and though they both nodded along as I explained that we'd be living here from now on, I'm pretty sure I'll have to explain it all again tomorrow.

By the time I'm done with their stories, they're both sleeping soundly, all tucked up in their new beds, in their new home. Downstairs, I find Greyson waiting for me in the living room with a glass of red wine.

"I could get used to this," I grin, taking the glass from him.

"Well, I wasn't sure if you'd want to stay up a while and have some wine, or if you'd like to... get an early night," he says, emphasizing the last part. The way he's looking at me, with a slight grin and hungry eyes, his implication is clear.

"Hmm," I reply, tapping my finger on my chin. "Tough call."

He arches his brows, amused. I think he knows that this conversation is only going to end one way.

"Just kidding," I beam, turning around and making a break for the stairs. "Race ya!"

I get as far as the landing. His thick arms scoop around my waist from behind, and he lifts me up and carries me into the master bedroom.

It's nothing like the bare, vacant room I left a couple of weeks ago. The paneling has been painted white, and the walls above it are sage green. There's a four-poster bed against the wall, draped with cream netting, and the bedding is shades of midnight blue and peach. I turn to face Greyson, and the surprise and delight of seeing this room for the first time must be all over my face because he's smiling with satisfaction as he watches me.

"Nice, huh?"

"Look at you, all proud of yourself," I grin, bopping him on the nose with my finger.

"Right, Ms. Brooks," he says, very seriously. "That's enough out of you."

He throws me down onto the bed, and I roll over to look up at him. I arch my back and waggle my brows at him, making an exaggerated show of trying to be sexy.

"*Bonjour*," I say, my voice low and husky.

He bursts out laughing and shakes his head at the absurdity of it, crawling on top of me as I giggle beneath him.

He takes my face in his hands like it's a fragile, precious thing, and presses gentle kisses onto my chin, my forehead, in a trail down my nose to the tip, and then, finally, after he's brushed his lips against mine and extracted a quiet whimper from them, he kisses my mouth.

He takes his time with me. His fingers are meticulous on the buttons of my jeans; his hands firm but gentle as they guide me out of my clothing. He pulls his shirt over his head and his mud-stained pants from his legs, and he poises himself over me again, his arms on either side of my head.

"Hey," I whisper.

He brushes a curl out of my face and runs his thumb across my mouth, then pulls my bottom lip down with just a little pressure, before releasing it to bounce back into place.

"Hey."

And then he pushes his hips between mine, parting my thighs wider, and presses naked sex against naked sex. I feel myself clench, my body alive with sudden, urgent desire. A smile sparkles in his eyes and he rolls his hips, teasing me, refusing to give me what I want, even as my hips roll up in response, reaching out for him.

"Do you want something, Allie?" he asks, with a wicked smirk.

"Everything," I breathe, barely able to put a coherent thought together.

He shifts himself down a little, then slowly brings his hips forward, sliding into me, filling me. I groan and wrap my legs around him, pulling him closer, insisting on more, and he obliges with the rhythmic thrusting of his hips.

He leans down to kiss me. His breathing is heavy, hot on my cheek, and he swallows the moans he draws out from my mouth.

He shifts, propping onto one elbow and sliding his other hand down, along my side, against my hips, and then into the nothing between us, and I know I'm done for.

His fingers move against me, urged on by the rhythm of his hips, circling, teasing until I am a muddled mess of moans and whimpers underneath him. He is a pent up animal, coiled like a spring, teetering on the edge of release. I feel the muscles of his back beneath the tips of my fingers, bunched and strained, and I hear the salacious slapping of our bodies echo back from the walls. We glisten in the moonlight, our bodies shimmering with sweat as we chase down ecstasy together.

I shatter in an explosive instant, rolling and moaning through wave after wave of pleasure, and as I ride my own euphoria I feel Greyson lose himself inside me.

He collapses on top of me, panting as hard as I am, and we float back to earth together.

❋

I lay beside Greyson, my head on his chest and one arm draped across his stomach, marveling at the fact that this is our bed. In our home. I still have to pinch myself whenever I think about everything that's happened today. The difference between how I felt just twenty-four short hours ago and how I feel now... it's like another lifetime.

"Allie," Greyson says, sitting up. I reluctantly slide off the spot on his chest that I was using as a pillow and look up at him.

"I have something for you."

That gets my attention. He's already given me so much today, I have a hard time believing there could be anything else.

"Oh?" I say, curiosity getting the better of me. "And what's that?"

His expression doesn't give much away, but there's a gravity about the way he's looking at me that makes me sit up and take notice.

Greyson kisses my cheek and rises, walks over to his discarded, muddy pants, and reaches into the pocket.

"I know we said we'd get a ring when the stores are open again," he says, turning around to face me.

"Yeeeeah," I say, questioningly. Where is this going?

He holds up his hand, and I see a handkerchief with the initials M. B. embroidered on the corner. I recognize it immediately. It's my Mom's.

"Well, we don't need to," he says, unfolding the last part of the handkerchief to reveal a ring.

I feel tears spring immediately to my eyes, and my face crumples with recognition. I clap a hand over my mouth, as much to stop myself from crying out as from surprise.

"Your mom says it was Libby's," he says. I nod my head quickly, my hand still covering my mouth. "And she said that you should have it."

The ring is polished gold with tiny diamonds sparkling around one side of it. It's been in my family for generations, passed down from eldest daughter to eldest daughter on their wedding day. Libby only got to wear it for two short years before she was taken from us.

Tears are streaming down my face. I know how gut-wrenching it must have been for my mother to make this gesture, acknowledging me as her eldest daughter now, opening the wound of Libby's loss once more.

Greyson gently pulls my hand from my mouth and kisses it.

"Alora Brooks," he says, for the second time today. "Will you marry me?"

I wipe the tears from my cheeks, smiling through them, and nod.

"Yes," I say. "Yes, I will."

He slides the ring onto my finger and leans in to kiss me.

We lay back down in our bed, and Greyson holds me close as he recounts the conversation he had with my mother in the hall. How she said she was so proud of me, and that Libby would be so happy with the way I'm raising the girls.

I pull his arms tighter around me, staring out the window as the stars twinkle over Sunrise Valley. I run my thumb over the metal band around my ring finger and sigh, barely able to believe everything that's happened in one short day. Or even in six short weeks.

The girls are just down the hall, sleeping soundly in their beds, and Greyson's breathing is getting slower as he starts to drift off, his nose buried in my hair.

"Hey, Greyson," I say, quietly.

"Mmm?" he murmurs.

"I love you."

I feel him smile against my hair, and he pulls me in tighter and kisses the back of my head.

"I love you, too."

EPILOGUE

Eighteen Months Later

Allie

I wake up and roll over, slinging my arm across the bed to pull myself closer to Greyson, only to find his side empty. It takes me a moment to remember what day it is, and why he's not there.

I can already hear movement downstairs, and the smell of coffee is wafting up through the house and into the master bedroom. When I hit the button on the side of my phone to bring it to life, I can see that it's just after 9 am.

"Shit!" I hiss and spring up out of bed.

I was sure I set my alarm for eight—but in all the excitement of last night, I must have forgotten.

"I slept late!" I say, a little panic in my voice, as I barrel into the kitchen.

Sadie is standing by the coffee machine, squinting at the little LCD screen as she waits for it to brew. Lottie and Emma are sitting at the table with Riley, Ethan and Emily's daughter, happily munching on some cereal.

"That's all right," says Sadie, cool as a cucumber. "You have hours yet. And besides, the extra rest will do you good."

"Good moooorning!" calls Sam as he enters the kitchen. He comes over to give me a quick squeeze, then we both perch ourselves on the stools at the breakfast bar and wait for Sadie to pour our coffee.

"One for you, Mary?" Sadie asks. I turn around to see my mom walking in, with River holding her hand.

"Oh, better not, dear," says Mom. "I'm already a bag of nerves."

"It's *me* that's getting married!" I grin at her.

"And you'll be wonderful," she replies, smiling. River skips over to help herself to some cereal, and Mom gives me a kiss on the cheek as she takes the stool beside mine.

"I made fruit salad," says Sadie, eyeing me. "As requested, to ward off any untimely food babies."

"What's a food baby?" asks Mom.

"It's when you eat lots of food and your belly does this!" says Sam, sticking out his gut as far as it will go. The girls at the table all giggle wildly at the sight.

We all eat breakfast together; the girls with their cereal, me and my mom (who is now adamantly avoiding a food baby herself) with our fruit salad, and Sadie and Sam tucking into eggs and toast.

When the hairdresser and the beautician arrive at the door, Sam decides to take his leave. He's part of my bridal party, but his suit—cut from the same vibrant pink silk as my bridesmaids' dresses—has been tailored at the same shop as Greyson and his groomsmen's suits. He's going to dress over at Eddie and Sadie's place with the rest of them and meet me at the church. I really can't wait to see him in a suit that's as flamboyant as he is.

I can't wait to see Greyson either, but whenever I think about him my tummy flips over, so I'm trying not to. Think about him, I mean. No point avoiding a food baby if you're just going to make yourself sick with butterflies instead!

It takes a few hours for my hair to be set and styled and my makeup to be professionally applied. By the time I'm done, Sadie and my mom have not only gotten dressed themselves but have also—miraculously—managed to herd the girls into their dresses as well.

My mom offers to keep an eye on the gaggle of tiny bridesmaids that are now running loose around the house, while Sadie and I head upstairs to get my dress on.

❄

"Thanks for doing this," I say to Sadie, once we're alone in the bedroom. I'm standing in front of a full-length mirror while Sadie straps me in.

"Helping you with your dress?" she asks.

"No. Being Maid of Honor. I know it's not your thing, but it means a lot."

"Are you kidding?" she asks, turning me around to face her. "Allie, I cannot think of a bigger honor in the entire world." She pauses for a moment, and a glimmer of sadness passes across her face.

"I know that it would have been... *should* have been Libby here, helping you into this dress." My eyes fall briefly downwards, and a pang shoots through my chest. "It means the world to me that you trust me to step into her shoes, even though I know I can't ever fill them. It's the best day of my life."

I smile at her through a haze of tears, and a lump lodges in my throat. She's right, it should have been Libby. But I couldn't ask for a better big-sister-in-law than Sadie.

"But don't tell your brother," she continues. "He thinks it's the second best." She winks at me and I laugh, my sorrow dissipating before any tears have a chance to leak out of my eyes and ruin my very expensive makeup.

She stands back and looks me up and down, and a satisfied smile creeps onto her face.

"Wow," she says. "Come on, let's go make your mom cry."

We're barely halfway down the stairs when we hear a loud BEEP outside, followed by the familiar BING BONG of the old doorbell echoing through the house. As we reach the bottom, my mom is just opening the door. It's my dad outside, come to ride with me to the church. They both look up and see me at the same time.

"Oh, my gosh," says my mom, clapping a hand over her mouth.

Her eyes are instantly full of tears, in probably the most predictable reaction ever. But I'm surprised by the quiver of my dad's lip as he looks me up and down.

"You look just wonderful, sweetheart," he says, his voice shaking.

I can feel that swirl of emotion building in my tummy again, welling up in my eyes, and I flap my hands in front of my face to try and stop myself from crying.

"Thanks, Dad. Are the cars ready?"

He nods. I grab my flowers from the table in the hallway and head outside with him. We climb into one car, and Sadie, Mom, and the girls climb into the other. As we pull away from the mansion, it occurs to me that the next time I set foot in it will be as a wife. Greyson's wife. I smile happily to myself at how natural it already feels to say that.

We're supposed to be married at 1 pm, so when we pull up outside the church at 1:02 the assistant pastor is outside, looking nervously at his watch.

"We're all ready for you!" he says as we get out of the car.

There's a flurry of activity as we get the girls in place. Sadie crouches down beside Emma, who's carrying her adorable little flower-girl basket by her side, and goes over the petal-sprinkling instructions for her, one last time.

Mom gives me a kiss and rushes off to take her seat in the church. I try to catch a glimpse inside, to see what I'm about to walk into. The place looks packed, but I can't really pick out anyone from here. I do see Ethan and Emily's son, Leo, just inside the door. He's nine years old now, but his little groomsman suit is obviously making him feel at least 12, given the way he's standing with his shoulders back and his chest puffed out.

I furrow my brow. There's no sign of the one person I'm expecting to see. "Where's Sam?" I ask, looking around.

"Here!" he says, looking more flustered than I've ever seen him as he appears around the corner.

My brow remains furrowed as he approaches. "Sam, where's your suit?" I ask. He's wearing the same rich navy that Greyson and all the other groomsmen are wearing, not the pink that I ordered for him.

He tries to whisper something to me, but the first notes of the bridal march pipe up from inside the church and drown him out. I guess that's the wedding equivalent of a starter's pistol because everyone suddenly springs into motion at once. My dad loops his arm through mine, Sadie sends Emma off to sprinkle her petals, the girls snap into formation, Sam gets into position in the bridal procession behind me... and we're off.

❄

Greyson

I look over at Ethan and he's looking right back at me, running his gaze all the way down to my feet and all the way back up again.

"Oh, shut up," I whisper as his lips start to twitch again.

"I can't," he says, his shoulders shaking with silent laughter.

"Some best man you are."

"Oh God," he whispers, and he lets out a weird choking noise as he tries to hold in his glee. "The pictures are going to be *amazing*."

I sigh.

It was Allie's bright idea—and I mean that literally, in every sense—to have Sam be a "bridesman" and wear a suit that matched the rest of her bridesmaids' dresses. And Sam was delighted—the prospect of wearing a flamboyantly pink suit to a wedding is right up his alley.

Unfortunately for me, and for the tailor who will soon be receiving the worst Yelp review in history, it is definitely not up *my* alley. But despite our best efforts to salvage the situation when the suits arrived with our measurements swapped, Sam was drowning in the pink and I couldn't squeeze my left thigh into the waistband of his pants. Eddie's jacket was way too short for me, and Ethan apparently has the shoulders of a gnat.

My options were to postpone the wedding, which was out of the question, or to take the L, wear this piece of art, and still get married to Allie today. So here I am. Standing in the church, about to marry the woman of my dreams… in a very skilfully-tailored pink suit.

A hush falls over the congregation as the pastor raises his arms for everyone to stand. The bridal march starts up and Ethan and I turn toward the pastor, who has been trying and failing not to stare at me since we showed up. I see little Emma from the corner of my eye as she lays down the last of her petals, just as she did in the rehearsal.

There is no such judgmental look in her eyes. She probably thinks this suit is the most amazing thing she has ever seen. She gives me a little wave, and I wink at her as she runs off to sit on the bride's side with Sadie's parents.

And then Allie steps into the room with her entourage, and my heart skips a beat. She looks absolutely radiant in her fitted ivory gown. But as she starts walking slowly down the aisle, and I can see her face more clearly, I know that we're in big trouble.

Her eyes are as wide and as round as saucers, and I can see a hollow in her throat where she's sucking it in to try and stop herself from laughing. Every few seconds, the urge to laugh seems to start getting the better of her and she has to look away—but then, as soon as it's passed, her eyes are drawn irresistibly back to the suit. Her father, walking arm-in-arm with her, looks absolutely bemused. He keeps squinting at me as though he thinks there must be something wrong with his eyes, like cataracts are the most reasonable explanation for why his future son-in-law appears to be standing on the altar in a pink suit.

Things only get worse as she reaches the altar and pulls up beside me. She is staring intensely, directly at my eyes to try and stop herself looking at the suit. The sheer struggle to keep it together is etched across her face, and I have very little confidence that she's going to be able to hold it in for this entire ceremony.

"Please be seated," says the pastor, as the music falls silent. "On behalf of Alora and Greyson—"

The first tiny snort escapes Allie's nose, and I hear another from Ethan behind me. I glance over to where Sadie is sitting with the other bridesmaids, and her entire face is squashed in on itself with the effort it's taking not to laugh.

The whole thing is ridiculous, and I can feel my own facade beginning to crack.

"I welcome you here today, and I would like to express on their behalf my gratitude for—"

She does it again. I pull my lips in between my teeth and bite on them from the inside, trying to ward off a laugh. From somewhere in the pews a little ways behind me, there's a quiet gasp, then a snicker.

Ethan can't hold it anymore. A long, loud snort comes out of him, and Allie loses control. Then Sadie, then Eddie, then Allie's parents. Like a dam bursting, the congregation dissolves into fits of laughter, one by one and then all at once, until I'm forced to give in and join them. Within a few seconds, the entire church is filled with uproarious laughter. Even the pastor is laughing.

"Oh my goodness!" cries Allie, with tears glittering along her lower lashes. "Look at you!"

"It was either this or wait," I grin. "And I'm not waiting!"

It takes five minutes and a few words from the pastor before the laughter eventually dies down and we can get on with the ceremony.

The service is beautiful, and in the end, it turns out that the mixup with the suits was a blessing in disguise. All the nervous energy in the room, the kind that people always feel at a wedding, simply evaporated as soon as we all started laughing together. By the time Allie and I are saying our vows, everyone is relaxed and happy.

"I now pronounce you man and wife," says the pastor, after I slip the ring onto Allie's finger. "You may kiss the bride."

I grab Allie and bend her backward, holding her securely in my arms, and press my lips to hers in front of all our witnesses. Our guests cheer and holler and clap, and I am the happiest man alive.

❄

Six Months after the Wedding

Greyson

It's a cold December afternoon, and I'm sitting in my office on a video call with Ethan. I haven't seen Allie yet today, but I presume she's in her studio working on this week's cartoon.

Her webcomic business really took off after the first couple of months. Now she sells merch and prints, and people pay her hundreds of dollars for commissioned caricatures.

"All right, we'll leave it there," says Ethan. "And we'll pick it up tomorrow. Enjoy your evening."

Pleasantries duly exchanged, we end the call.

The girls are due home from school soon, which means that Allie will be coming back up to the house from her studio in the outbuilding. I pick up my empty mug from beside the wedding photo on my desk and grin when I catch sight of the fuchsia suit. I was so pissed when I realized I had to wear it, but it ended up making the best day of my life even more memorable. I can't even look at it now without smiling.

"Hey," I say, walking into the kitchen. Allie is standing near the counter with her back to me. She doesn't say anything, or even turn around to greet me, which is highly unusual for her.

"Knock, knock!" calls Sadie as she pushes the front door open to drop the kids home. "I can't stay," she continues, turning back towards the door as soon as the girls are safely inside. "Kids in the car. See you tomorrow!"

I notice Allie slip something into her pocket, and when she turns around there is a lingering look of shock on her face.

But as soon as the girls come barreling in, it's replaced by a bright smile that she beams toward them.

"Hey!" she says, reaching down to hug them both tight.

"Daddy, look!" Emma beams excitedly, rushing over to me with a piece of paper in her hand. I pluck her up from the ground and look at the picture, tapping my chin as I give it the consideration it deserves.

"Hmmm, yes… I love what you've done with the blue," I say of the multicolor squiggles on the page, and she gives me a wide grin.

"All right, girls, you know the drill," says Allie. "Upstairs, drop your bags off in your room, and wash your hands!"

The girls stampede up the stairs, and we're suddenly alone again.

"Everything all right?" I ask Allie. She really seemed distracted before the girls came in. I'm starting to get a bit worried.

She looks up at me, chewing one side of her bottom lip, and nods.

I arch my brow. "Uh, okay. Are you sure? Because you're being kinda weird."

She nods again, then walks over to me and reaches into her pocket. When she pulls her hand out again, she's holding an unassuming little white stick. She holds it out for me to take it.

It takes me a while to realize what it is, and a while longer to realize that she wouldn't have given me a pregnancy test if it had come back negative.

"Oh my God," I say, looking at her.

She has tears in her eyes and a smile growing steadily on her lips.

"Really?" I ask, my heart speeding up in my chest.

She nods again.

Fireworks of joy explode inside me and I grab her up and spin her around, laughing.

"What are you laughing for, Daddy?" asks Lottie. She and Emma have returned from their rooms and they're standing in the doorway, looking at us like we've gone mad.

I put Allie down, and she takes my hand and calls the girls over to the table.

"Let's sit down," she says, lacing her fingers between mine. "We have something to tell you."

WANT MORE?

If you loved Allie and Greyson and you're not ready to say goodbye, you can pick up a FREE short story about them by signing up to my mailing list!

ABOUT THE AUTHOR

Harmony Knight loves reading great romance books, drinking tea, and writing bios in third person.

She was born and raised in an ex-mining village in South Wales (UK), but after kissing her fair share of frogs she found her prince and moved across the Irish Sea. She now lives in Ireland with her family.

Harmony writes the books she loves to read, full of loveable heroines and the caring alpha men who have to have them, and she hopes you'll love to read them, too!

For news and updates, check out her website at www.harmonyknight.com or you can sign up for her mailing list so you'll never miss a release!

Printed in Great Britain
by Amazon